Common Enemy

by

Sandra Dailey

This is a work of fiction. Names, characters, places, and incidents are either the product of the author's imagination or are used fictitiously, and any resemblance to actual persons living or dead, business establishments, events, or locales, is entirely coincidental.

Common Enemy

COPYRIGHT © 2014 by Sandra Dailey

Cover Art by *Debbie Taylor*

The Wild Rose Press, Inc.
PO Box 708
Adams Basin, NY 14410-0708
Visit us at www.thewildrosepress.com

Publishing History
First Crimson Rose Edition, 2014
Print ISBN 978-1-62830-327-8
Digital ISBN 978-1-62830-328-5

Published in the United States of America

"Did you love him?"

"I thought I did, a long time ago. That didn't last long." Jordan sniffed and wiped her eyes. "He was an animal. All he cared about was taking whatever he wanted and destroying everything else. I got the worst of both. When he was mad, it was really bad. When he was happy, it was even worse."

She couldn't look him in the eye. He understood what she was saying and it made his skin crawl. He hated this guy worse now than he had six years ago. What kind of hell had the man put Jordan through?

He lowered himself onto the sofa with her in his arms. They clung to each other for several minutes.

"God, what a pair we are," he scoffed. "Both of us were victims of the same monster."

"When were you in Tampa?" she asked. Bobby Ray had never gone far from the area.

"I was born and raised in Tampa. My parents and brother still live there." He knew she really wanted to know when he'd been attacked. He ran his finger down the scar on his cheek. "This happened six years ago. They didn't try to make it pretty, because they didn't think I'd live. I was in a coma when they found me. They thought I'd probably suffered extensive brain damage from the beating. I have more scars."

"I know," she admitted. "I saw you out the window the second day you were here. Can you tell me what happened?"

Dedication

I'm dedicating this book to my son.
Like a warrior's sword, he was forged in fire,
tested on the field, and came out strong.

I love you, Evan

Chapter One

The sun dipped low behind the old farmhouse setting it in silhouette against the evening sky. Jordan parked and got out to look closer. Her heart sank when its condition became clear. She certainly had her work cut out for her. The blue paint on the two-story structure had faded to gray and was peeling in large patches. The windows were covered in mossy grime. Some of the shutters were barely hanging onto the building. A few shingles were missing from the roof. But as always, the pair of wooden rocking chairs stood guard by the front door.

Mr. Coleman had walked over from his farm and was sweeping clouds of dust from the front porch. He was the nearest neighbor and Gram's best friend. He'd been with Gram when she'd suffered a stroke and had kept an eye on her property until her recent death.

"I'm sorry the old place is in such a state, Jordan. I should have kept it up better for you. I'm just not as young as I used to be. Your grandmother would have a flip tizzy if she could see how it looks." He squinted to watch a second car stop behind Jordan's. It was Holly Douglas, her childhood friend.

"Its okay, Mr. Coleman," Jordan assured him. "I've got plenty of time to put it right. I'm just glad to be home."

"I was hoping you'd feel that way. I hate the

thought of the old place being sold to strangers."

"Thank you." Jordan gave him a hug, and then took another look around. "I'll have to hire someone to help me with the heavy work. I had no idea the house had gotten so run down. Do you know anyone I could call?"

"I've got a man that helped me rebuild my barn. We had a lot of damage after the last hurricane and he was a godsend. I hated to see him go, but I didn't have anything left for him to do at my place. He's a nice, quiet guy, and does excellent work, but he's a drifter. His name is Conner McCrae and he works real cheap. I've already asked him to come by tomorrow."

"Do you really think that's a good idea?" Holly asked from behind Jordan. "She and her daughter, Lizzy, will be living way out here alone. What do you know about this man?"

"He gave me a list of people he'd done work for that all sang his praises. I guess he fell on hard times a few years back. Now he just stays to himself and does what he can to get by, but he puts in a hard day's work. I've gotten to know him and I'd trust him with my life. I'm only a half-mile down the road if you need me, but I know he won't give you any trouble. You won't find a better worker." Arnold leaned the old broom in its place at the end of the porch. "I'd better start back home before it gets any later." He tipped his old straw hat. "Good night ladies."

As Holly helped Jordan unload her car, she told her about her husband and two sons. She talked about her job at the local grocery and the upcoming Heritage Day celebration in the park. It was nice to reconnect with her old school pal after seven long years, but the trip from Tampa and Gram's funeral had worn Jordan out.

She couldn't hold back a big yawn.

"I have to get back home," Holly groaned. "Charlie must be going crazy with the boys by now. Promise you'll call as soon as they get the phone turned on tomorrow. I want to have you over for a barbeque soon. It's Charlie's specialty."

"I'd love to," Jordan exclaimed. "I can't wait to meet your family. Just give me a couple of weeks, though. I have to put some serious work into this house and I need a little time to adjust."

"Would you like me to come over in the morning when you meet Mr. Coleman's handyman? I still feel a little uncomfortable about you being alone out here with him."

"No, I'll be fine. Mr. Coleman wouldn't send anyone over who he didn't trust completely. Besides that, you have to go to work tomorrow. I'll see you when I come into town to do some grocery shopping."

Jordan walked upstairs and fell into bed exhausted, physically and mentally. Being in Gram's house again brought back so many memories. This had been her first real home. Her mother had dropped her off here when she was seven. One day when Jordan was in the sixth grade, she'd come home to find a man sitting with her grandparents. He was rolling his hat in his hands, staring at the floor while Gram cried and Pop stared into the fireplace looking devastated. Her mother had been found in an Atlanta hotel room, dead from a drug overdose. Jordan hadn't known how to feel about it. She didn't really know her mother. Her grandparents were her family and this was her home. She had been happy here.

Jordan drifted off to sleep for what seemed like a

few minutes.

"Mom, mom, mom, mom…"

Jordan opened one eye to find Lizzy lying beside her, her face a mere three inches away. She lifted herself on one elbow to see the alarm clock over her daughter's head. It was eight o'clock. She flopped on her back, waiting for the fuzziness in her head to clear. It took a moment to realize that she was lying in her grandmother's bed, in her grandmother's house.

For the first time in years, she'd slept through the night without waking at every little sound. She hadn't jumped from the bed with a feeling of stark fear. She and her daughter were safe.

"What's for breakfast, Mommy? I'm starving." Lizzy squirmed out of her embrace and off the bed. She stood in her pink nightgown and bare feet, her copper colored hair, in tangles, caught the sunlight. Jordan could see the dusting of freckles over the little girl's nose. She had always hated her own auburn hair and freckles, but they were adorable on Lizzy.

"One of Gram's friends sent a coffee cake yesterday, but I don't have any milk. Would you like to have a cup of tea with me, like a big girl?"

"Well, I guess, but just this once. It's not really good for me you know."

"I know, but I promise that I'll get you some milk when I go to the store."

Lizzy jumped from the bed to run out of the room. She stopped in the hall and yelled back, "Do you think the man outside will want some tea, too, Mommy?"

"What man?"

"The man under your car," Lizzy answered matter-of-factly as she ran on ahead.

Jordan finished fastening the snap on her jeans before she opened the front door. And yes, a man was just coming out from under her car. Even with his back to her, she knew she'd never seen him before. Not a lot of men were that much taller than her. Not many men had hair almost as long as hers. His was blond and braided halfway down his muscular back. His fists at the waist of his tight black T-shirt showed off the bulging muscles in his arms. The faded jeans were snug over well-shaped legs. And it was all topped by a well-worn straw cowboy hat. Nope, she would have definitely remembered him. The stranger alert in her head went off like fourth-of-July fireworks.

"If you're checking for a low-jack, I have to warn you…that car is not worth the trouble of stealing." Sarcasm was her first shield of defense.

He looked over his shoulder with a smile that revealed even white teeth and light blue eyes in contrast to his darkly tanned skin. "I was trying to see what's leaking under there. I think you may have a problem."

"Oh great!" Jordan stomped down the steps. "That's just what I need right now!" She stopped beside him and contemplated the puddle under the front half of her car.

"Well, don't worry." He kept his head down and his hat low. "I do cars as well as houses and lawn work. Looks like you could use all my services. This place is a mess."

"You must be the man that Mr. Coleman told me about. If you're trying to charm me into hiring you, you've gotten off to a damn good start."

"Sorry, but I call 'em as I see 'em. I heard that the place had been empty for a few years and it shows."

"I didn't expect you so early. We haven't even had breakfast yet."

"Hey, mister, you want some tea?" Lizzy bounded down the steps in her nightgown. She lost her footing on the bottom step and pitched forward onto the dirt path. The man's reflexes were faster than Jordan's. As he picked Lizzy up his hat fell behind him. He stood her in front of him to dust away the dirt and inspect the scrape on her knee.

"How'd you get that big scar on your face?" Lizzy blurted.

"I got cut with a knife, but it wasn't nearly as bad as falling from the porch steps. You must be a very brave girl."

"I am. How did you get cut with a knife? Mom doesn't let me touch knives."

"Lizzy, don't be so nosy." By this time Jordan had recovered from the shock of seeing the deep scar. It ran down the man's left cheek, into his short beard, and under the collar of his shirt.

"It's okay. Kids are always curious. It's best to let them ask." He picked up his hat and hit it against his leg to knock off the dirt before he put it back on. He turned back to her daughter. "You know Lizzy, it doesn't really matter how it happened. It just shows you how dangerous knives can be. I guess it'll be a good idea to listen to your mom about that kind of stuff."

"I do," Lizzy replied. "What's your name?"

"I'm Connor McCrae. I came by to talk to your mom. But first she needs to make you some breakfast while I look at her car."

"Okay!" Lizzy ran back up the steps.

"Hey! Slow down before you scuff your other

knee." He watched her with a smile. To Jordan he said, "That little girl must be a handful."

"I'm Jordan Holbrook." As she shook his hand she sized him up and figured him to be about six-feet-five. Up close he didn't look too much older than her. "Thanks for being so nice to Lizzy. She can be a bit forward sometimes. I hope she didn't say anything to embarrass you."

"Of course not. She's a great kid." He held his hand out. "Give me your keys and I'll look at the car while you eat. I should have an idea about the rest of the work to be done around here soon, too."

Jordan watched Connor walk around the house and property most of the day. She tried to keep her mind on her own work, but it was disconcerting to have a stranger on the premises conducting a silent inspection.

Lizzy had spent the day putting her room in order and had stayed out of the way, for the most part.

When the kitchen had been scrubbed to her satisfaction, Jordan realized that it was getting dark. She folded the dishtowel over the oven handle and walked upstairs to take a shower. She was exhausted. Lizzy had fallen asleep just after dinner. It was time to pamper herself for a little while.

****

Bobby Ray Butler watched the sunset through the barred window of his prison cell. He squinted as the florescent lights automatically came on. At nine o'clock they'd turn off again to leave him in darkness. It had been the same for the last five years, five months and twenty days.

He'd worn the same orange jumpsuits every one of those days. He'd eaten the same tasteless food and walked the same exercise yard. Any time he was outside his cell, he'd had to watch his back. The bad guys here were dirty, diseased, and mean. The good guys fell to them or learned to be just as bad. Bobby Ray had gone to great lengths to avoid all but a select few.

He earned a miniscule amount of money working on the grounds. Almost every dime of it had gone into pads of paper. The only time his mind was truly calm were the hours he spent sketching his pictures.

He peeled a picture from the wall where it hung from a small piece of tape he'd had to beg for. He'd never beg for anything again. The circumstance that put him here wasn't right. A man should be able to trust his wife. King of his castle and all that crap.

He lifted another picture from the collage on his wall. He'd be getting out soon and wouldn't leave a single one behind. No one here deserved to even look at them.

He'd been through hell, but soon it would be his turn to send someone else. The difference was, her hell would be permanent. There'd be no reprieve, no escape, and no second chance.

****

Connor came into contact with Jordan several times that day. He liked what he saw. She had to be almost six-feet-tall and all woman. Not the skinny kind of girl who giggled a lot, but a real woman.

He could tell she'd just gotten out of bed when they first met. There was nothing to compare with a woman who looked that good first thing in the morning. Her messy hair hung to her waist. It shined like a new penny in the sun. Her chocolate colored eyes sat over lightly freckled cheeks. She had a straight thin nose that led to pretty, coral colored lips. The big T-shirt she'd worn revealed full breasts on a sturdy frame. She wasn't heavy, but athletic. The kind of woman you just dreamed of holding onto all night long.

She was the kind of woman who deserved a good-looking man. Not a freak like him. It had probably taken all the willpower she had to look at him. If she weren't alone and in need of a lot of help, he would just fire up his van and save her the misery.

Connor sat in the open back door of his van eating stew from a can that he'd heated over a propane burner. He should have driven into town to have a decent meal at the diner. He didn't like the idea of leaving the woman and child alone when they'd barely arrived. All they'd brought with them was what they'd packed in a car. So far, they were living on leftovers from a funeral reception. At least the house was still fully furnished. They had good beds to sleep in.

He was getting tired of living out of the confines of the old Dodge, but that was what his life had come to. He could hardly remember what it felt like to sleep in a normal bed. Would the nightmares still plague him every night in a real bed?

His eyes moved over the side of the house and up to the second floor windows. She was sitting in her room, brushing her hair. The name Jordan suited her. He liked it.

He imagined himself in that window standing behind Jordan. He would brush her hair aside and place a soft kiss on the curve of her neck and gaze into the mirror to meet her eyes. For a moment they would still be closed as she took a long breath. Then her eyes would open and she would look back at him. What would he see in those beautiful brown eyes, pity or revulsion?

Connor threw the half-eaten can of stew into the trashcan before he pulled his legs up and slid the door shut, blocking out the view. What had he been thinking? He'd never be able to have a woman like her.

Chapter Two

Jordan heard the slide and click of the van's door against the silence outside. She hadn't realized Connor was still out there. The old van looked dark and lonely in the dim moonlight. She hadn't seen him around the house since nightfall. She'd assumed that he'd gone home. Mr. Coleman had said he was a drifter. Perhaps that van was his home. He must be so lonely in such cramped quarters, but lonely was lonely no matter where you were. Would he be any lonelier than her tonight?

She slid under the covers and snuggled her pillow, alone. Why couldn't love be like they showed in the movies, or wrote in books? She imagined the feel of a hard, warm chest under her hands. She could almost hear a strong heartbeat under her ear. He would bring his folded arms down from behind his head to circle them around her. She pictured that battered old cowboy hat resting in the chair across the room.

Jordan sat up and shook the images from her mind. If she kept up this fantasy, she wouldn't be able to face him in the morning.

The next thing she knew, Jordan woke to the ringing of her new telephone. The bedside clock read 9:15. Lizzy didn't usually sleep so late. She quickly pulled jeans on under her nightshirt and went to the table in the hallway. As her hand touched the receiver she remembered that she hadn't called Holly to give her the new number. She hadn't called anyone.

"Hello?"

"Are you and your little girl all settled in, Jordan?" a low male voice asked.

"Who is this?" Jordan's heart started pounding so hard her chest ached.

"I'll be watching you," the man added. "I wouldn't get too comfortable if I were you."

When the dial tone indicated the caller had hung up, she lowered the receiver back onto its cradle with a shaky hand. Bobby Ray was still in prison. It had only been a horrible joke. She had to believe that or go back to the insanity of her past.

From the bottom of the stairs she saw movement on the front porch. Then she heard the sound of Lizzy's voice. Lizzy was outside with someone! Fear tightened in her stomach as she took the steps two at a time. She found Lizzy and Connor sitting in the old rocking chairs. On an upturned crate were a quart of milk and a box of donuts.

"What's going on out here? You can't just abduct my daughter and give her this-this junk food." Jordan scowled.

"She came to me," Connor stated. "She said you didn't have any milk. I figured, as long as I was going to town anyway, I'd load her up with sugar, too, just to keep you on your toes. I also got the parts for your car so stop being so grumpy." He looked down at Lizzy. "Jeez, does she always wake up like that?"

"No. Sometimes she doesn't even wait to get dressed." Lizzy giggled with chocolate-coated lips.

"I don't need you two ganging up on me this early.

I'll talk to you after I've had a cup of coffee." She brushed back the hair that had fallen into her eyes.

"Are you okay?" Connor asked. "You're shaking like a leaf."

"Of course I'm okay. It just scared me when I woke and found my five-year-old daughter outside." She gripped Lizzy's hand and pulled her to the door. "Don't ever do that again, young lady. From now on you're to wake me before you go downstairs."

"I'm sorry, Mommy," Lizzy cried.

An hour later, Jordan had calmed her ragged nerves. She walked out to the porch to find Conner was sitting in the same chair as before with a cup of coffee and a notepad in his hand.

"Are you ready to give me the bad news?" she asked.

****

"It's not as bad as it looks." He snuck a nervous glance her way. "The house is sound, good foundation, plumbing, wiring, and roof. I didn't find any infestation or mold, which is amazing in this area, especially after the house has been closed up for so long. It needs work, but actually, your car is in worse shape than the house. Your water pump is shot and the hoses look like they could split at any moment. I'll have to replace the antifreeze, too. You shouldn't drive it until I'm finished. You'd be stranded on the side of the road. I guess that should be the first thing I work on."

"I need the car, living way out here. I'll give you the money for the parts you bought. Can you pick up some groceries in town before you get started? I just have a short list."

"I guess I can do anything you like if I'm working

for you." He peeked out from under the brim of his hat again.

"But, you haven't told me what the house needs yet."

"You need new caulking around the windows, new paint inside and out. A good chimney sweep, repairs on the existing shingles and shutters, better locks on the doors, a security system—"

"Hold up a minute. A security system? This is our home, not a fortress."

"Welcome to the twenty-first century," he laughed. "If you were to have any trouble out here, who would know? I really think it's something you should consider. I bet half the people in town know you live here alone. I don't imagine you have gossips in a town this size, do you? Besides that, it would let you know if Lizzy escapes again."

Her brow furrowed with indecision, but she hung on to her tough stubbornness…just barely.

"I'll think about it, but we've never had any problems here before. I grew up in this town. It's always been a safe place."

Connor decided to leave that idea for another time and went back to his list. "The barn is in really bad shape. You could do an awful lot with a space that size. We'll talk about it after the necessary things are done. I just can't see how it got so bad, though, considering how the rest of the house was kept."

"My pop, I mean grandfather, used to write his column for the paper out there. That's where he was when he died twelve years ago." She looked out at the barn with a haunted expression. "Gram couldn't make herself go in there much after that. It was a really special place for them."

"I was sorry to hear about your grandmother. I heard she was quite a special lady."

"Thank you." Jordan smiled. "Mr. Coleman must have told you that. I think he was sweet on her."

They both fell quiet for a few moments. Finally, Jordan asked, "What are you going to charge me for this work?"

"I can't lie to you, ma'am. Materials aren't cheap."

"I worked for a construction company for the last seven years," Jordan said. "I know exactly how much materials cost. I want to know what your fees are."

He looked down at his feet. This was the deal breaker. "I live in my van. I could park it behind the barn, or wherever you want. I work from sunup to sundown, no Sundays. After work I could use a place to shower and a good meal. Besides that, I would need about fifty dollars a week for gas and such. I'd stay out of your way, but I would be here until I know that you and Lizzy are safe and sound. It may take a few months."

"Mr. Coleman tells me you have references."

"You're a smart lady. You must take after your grandmother."

"What makes you say that?"

"I've seen her house." He rose and hopped down the porch steps.

Something was wrong in this house. He'd seen the haunted eyes and defensive body language before. Ms. Jordan Holbrook had secrets she wasn't sharing. The question was, how involved did he want to get? He had plenty of problems of his own.

****

That evening Connor had finished repairing the car. He had even changed the oil and filters. Jordan watched him from the kitchen window as he washed his hands with a bar of soap and the garden hose. To her surprise, he pulled his T-shirt off and sprayed the water down over his head. As he stretched to let the water cascade down his body, she saw the scar that crossed the left side of his massive chest and another across his stomach. Whoever hurt him had intended to kill. Her heart ached for the pain it must have caused him. Still the ropes of muscle and light covering of honey colored hair on his body fascinated her. If she were in the market for a man, he would definitely fit the bill. However, a man was the last thing she needed.

A half hour later, he walked through the back door dressed in the dirty T-shirt again with a small bundle of clothes wrapped in a towel. "Is it okay to use your shower now?"

"Sure." She smiled. "Help yourself. Dinner will be ready by the time you're finished."

"I generally take my dinner to the van to eat. I don't want to get in your way."

"Lizzy's been looking forward to having company. She had to leave all her friends when we moved. It would mean an awful lot to her if you'd stay."

"I guess it would be okay for today, if you're sure you don't mind."

Connor returned to the kitchen a short time later looking fresh and smelling of soap. He set his bundle of dirty clothes on the floor next to the back door. He looked over at Jordan pouring milk into glasses on the table as Lizzy waited impatiently to begin eating. He hesitated for a moment before removing his hat and placing it on top of the bundle. A place was set for him across from Jordan with Lizzy between them. It had been so long since he'd had a home cooked meal with a family. He hoped he would remember how to behave.

"Mom always lets me say grace before we eat." Lizzy's little fingers closed around his and Jordan reached out for his other hand. As they touched he felt a skip in his heartbeat, he looked up to see Jordan's eyes on his. Both of them looked away instantly. At the end of Lizzy's childlike prayer she added, "Thank you for sending Connor to be our friend. Amen."

Lizzy did most of the talking during dinner. Connor responded to her with short answers, watching his plate. When the meal was over, he offered to help with the dishes.

"I don't have anything to do tonight but the dishes," Jordan told him. "Please don't take away my night's entertainment. As a matter of fact, you could leave those clothes by the washing machine."

"I usually take them to the Laundromat in town on Sunday. I can't have you washing my clothes. It wouldn't be right. I work for you."

"You know I could be paying someone else a whole lot more to do the same work you're doing. Don't argue with me on this. I have to run that washing machine anyway. Your clothes won't be any trouble. And, like you said, I'm the boss".

"Yes, ma'am." Connor shrugged and tipped his hat before leaving.

Chapter Three

The whole first week was filled with hard work. Jordan scrubbed down each and every room. Her grandmother's clothes and personal items were donated to the church. Her papers were sorted and filed. It was a sentimental experience, pieces of her childhood hidden in every closet and corner. The trip down memory lane caused a rollercoaster of emotions. She'd laugh when she found little clay pots and crayon drawings from grade school. She'd cried when she found one of Gram's earrings or lace handkerchiefs. Inside the bible was a picture of her grandparents looking into each other's eyes on the day they were married. She wondered if she would ever feel the love she saw between the two of them.

Jordan set the picture out where Lizzy could see it. Maybe someday it would bring her the luck that Jordan and her mother had never had. She propped the picture against the wall on the table at the end of the hall. The telephone by her hand rang and startled her.

"Hello?"

"Hello, Jordan. I just wanted to let you know I'm still watching."

"Why are you doing this? Who are you?"

The line went dead.

It was the same man who'd called before. It had to be a prank. Bobby Ray was still behind bars. He had no idea where she was.

Maybe it was a kid with a mature voice, but how did he know her name? Her number wasn't published. Maybe it was someone she'd known in school. She scanned her memories to come up with anyone who'd given her a hard time back then, but couldn't think of a single person.

The only people who had her number were Mr. Coleman and Holly. Mr. Coleman was a private person. He'd rather die than give anyone information about her. She'd ask Holly after her friend got off work tonight. When she found out who was harassing her, they'd have hell to pay.

****

Now that the car was finished, Connor set to work on the lawn. He was afraid of the creatures that could be concealed under the tall weeds and debris. Lizzy needed a safe place to play. This part of Florida could hide snakes, rats, and even small alligators. The trees and shrubs were cut back and shaped. The flowerbeds were edged and filled with colorful annuals. Already it was starting to look brighter. He couldn't resist hanging a wood plank swing from the magnolia tree in the back yard.

Jordan and Connor stayed to themselves until dinnertime when Lizzy insisted he eat with them. He and Jordan were quietly polite to each other. Both enjoyed Lizzy's animated tales of her daily adventures.

After helping him carry a sofa out to the lawn on Friday morning, Jordan flopped down on it exasperated. "I don't know how I'm going to get all of this stuff clean again. Everything is so full of dust it's falling apart. Nothing had been covered to protect it before

Gram left. She probably didn't realize she'd never be coming back. I don't even know if it can be recovered."

"Why don't you just replace it?" Connor asked. "If money is a problem, we could look at some secondhand stuff that's in better shape than this, and it would probably be newer."

"I could never do that." Jordan looked at him as if he had lost his mind. "These are Gram's things. They belong in her house."

"Do you mean to say your grandmother never replaced any of her furniture? Was all this here when she moved in?" Connor fought to suppress a smile.

"Well, of course not. As a matter of fact, I remember her redecorating the whole house a few times while I lived here."

"What do you suppose she would do with this stuff if she were here now?" he asked.

"She'd probably drag it all out to the center of the yard and set fire to it."

"But you think she'd be offended if you don't keep it forever?"

"I didn't say forever."

"This is your house now. She gave it to you. She wants you to be happy in it. Keep the pictures and books and china, but let the rest go. We're going to paint every room anyway. We may as well go all the way with this makeover. Can you afford to make a few changes?"

"You'd be surprised what I can afford," Jordan scoffed. "Gram left me enough money to live on for years. However, I plan to get a job when Lizzy starts school. I'm not a lazy person." She frowned in thought at her folded hands. "You know something? You're right. Let's go shopping!"

"I have work to get done."

"Who's the boss, Connor?" She narrowed her eyes.

"You're the boss." He bowed and smiled.

On the way to town, they discussed the items that could be kept. Tables and bookshelves, bed frames and dressers. At the hardware store, they pored over paint samples and supplies. They systematically planned each room in the downstairs area of the house. After picking out drapes and rugs, they moved on to furniture. Finally, Jordan was satisfied for the day. "While you finish setting up the deliveries, I'm going to pop over to the grocery and say hello to a friend."

****

Jordan found Holly stocking canned goods on a shelf at the back of the store.

"You sure look a whole lot better then you did last week," Holly remarked. "I guess you're settling into the old house all right. Can you bring Lizzy over for that barbeque this weekend? Maybe I can have Charlie invite one of the guys from work, if you're interested in meeting someone."

"I'm only interested in meeting your husband and sons. All other men are out of the question."

Lizzy tugged on her sleeve. "What about Connor? He's a man."

"Who's Connor?" Holly asked with a sly smile.

"He's the handyman Mr. Coleman sent over. He really is a godsend. He fixed my car and cleared the lawn. He's in the middle of getting the outside of the house ready to paint. Today we're shopping for the things we need inside. We're just doing the downstairs for now. I'm totally exhausted."

"He sounds like quite a man."

"He is," Lizzy chimed in again. "He's my friend and he eats dinner with us every night."

"Maybe you should bring him along this weekend."

"I could ask him, but I wouldn't expect him to come." Jordan shrugged. "He's really shy about being around strangers."

"Well that's just silly. No one stays shy around my tribe for long."

"I guess he doesn't feel that he looks presentable."

"Do you feel that way about him?" Holly asked.

"Of course not."

"Well, you can ask him anyway and call me when you know. Everyone is welcome. Maybe I could have him look at a few things around my house. Charlie is a wizard on the barbeque grill, but he's no good with tools."

"I'll call you." Jordan ushered Lizzy toward the cashier.

****

Connor had stayed behind at the furniture store arranging delivery dates and giving directions to the house. The shipping department was at the back of the store at the big bay doors that led out to the alley. On an impulse, Connor took a shortcut through the alley to get to the grocery.

Three young punks wearing old leather jackets were hiding behind a dumpster. The smell of marijuana was strong. The smallest of the group had spiked black hair. The other two must have been brothers. Both looked like underage wrestlers with shaved heads. They were laughing at a dirty white plastic bag lying on the ground. The bag moved.

"What's in the bag, boys?" Connor scowled at them.

"What's it to you, Frankenstein?" The smaller boy wasn't intimidated, and his friends laughed harder.

"Give me the bag."

"If you want it, get it yourself." One of the others boys kicked it away.

"Give me the bag," he repeated.

"You think we're scared of you just because you're big and ugly? You can't take all of us on," the third boy boasted.

"I don't intend to. I intend to beat the shit out of you and your brother."

"Oh yeah? What am I supposed to be doing while you do that?" said the smallest.

Connor looked him in the eye. "You're what I intend to beat them with."

The laughing stopped.

The door across the alley opened from the beauty salon. A big buxom blonde woman walked out. "Hey! Aren't you two boys the Donahue twins? Your momma is coming in tomorrow to have her hair done. I'll be sure to tell her that I saw you. I'll be sure to tell her what I smelled out here, too."

"We were just taking a shortcut home. We're not doing anything," one said as they turned and jogged away.

"So what's going on here?" The woman gazed at the remaining boy.

"I was thinking of taking this boy out for a good beating," Connor replied.

"That sounds like a great idea. I'll forget I saw you,

just in case they look for witnesses later."

The remaining boy looked at each of them in panic and ran.

"You're one mean son-of-a-bitch, McCrae." The woman laughed.

"How do you know me?" Connor knelt to untie the plastic bag.

"I'm a friend of old man Coleman. Don't judge me. Even old geezers like him need companionship on occasion. He told me about you." She held her hand out to shake his. "My name is Joyce Walker. So, what's in the bag?"

"Looks like a kitten. I don't think they had a chance to hurt it. Sure is dirty. Smells like pot too."

"Give me that thing while it's still mellowed out. I'll be back in ten minutes."

She returned with a clean fluffy tabby. "Here you go."

"What am I supposed to do with it?"

"You're the hero. You'll figure it out."

Before Connor walked away, he had to ask, "How did you know how to handle those boys?"

"You've never met Mrs. Donahue. She looks just like her boys but with more hair...and a whole lot bigger."

On the way home Jordan chatted on and on about the plans for the house. Connor nodded and tried to pretend he was listening. In his mind, he kept playing back the scene in that alley, the words ugly and Frankenstein ringing in his head. He reminded himself he shouldn't let the punks, high on pot, bother him. The truth was, they did. Those boys were uninhibited by the dope. They just said what they saw. That's how most people saw him. He realized Jordan had asked a question.

"I'm sorry. I was distracted. What did you say?"

"I said, are you okay? You're staring out the window rubbing your stomach."

"Oh, I forgot." He unbuttoned his plaid shirt and pulled out the kitten. He jumped when Jordan and Lizzy squealed loudly.

"It's so cute. Where did you get it?" Jordan asked.

"I found it. Thought it might grow into a pretty good mouser."

"What's his name? Is he a boy?" Lizzy asked.

Taking a quick look, Connor said, "Yep, looks like he's a tom."

"I like the name Tom. Can we keep him in the house?"

"It's Connor's cat, not ours. He'll want to keep it with him," Jordan replied.

"I don't get too many mice in my van, but it's your call."

"Well, if you're sure, I guess it'll be okay to let Lizzy take care of him."

That night at dinner Lizzy told Connor about their invitation to the Douglas's for a barbeque.

"That sounds like fun," Connor said.

"You're coming too, aren't you?" Lizzy silently pleaded with puppy dog eyes.

"Nope, I think I'll go fishing."

"Well then, I'm going fishing too. Do you want to come with us Mommy?"

"No honey. I already told Miss Holly that I'd come to her house. You should come too. She has two little boys for you to make friends with." She turned to

Connor. "She did say you were welcome to come if you'd like."

"Boss, I think socializing with your friends on the weekend is stepping a little over the line."

"Connor is already my friend. How is he going to eat if we're not here?" Lizzy was near tears.

"Calm down, Lizzy." Connor gently rubbed her head. "I ate for a long time before I started working here. I can make do on my own just fine. Now, you need to make friends with other kids. They'll go to your school, and they can help you out. I can't go to school with you, you know. I think it's important that you meet these guys. Besides that, you can't make your mom go all by herself, can you?"

"I guess not," Lizzy pouted.

"You're better with Lizzy than I am," Jordan said after her daughter had left the table. "It almost makes me jealous."

"I'm thinking she may be getting too attached to me. It might be better if I didn't spend so much time with her."

"I have to admit the same thing crossed my mind. It'll break her heart though. I don't know if I can handle that right now. She's already been through so much. Maybe after she meets more people she won't be so attracted to you."

Connor was surprised by her choice of words. How could she think anyone would be attracted to him? The phone rang.

"Aren't you going to answer that?"

"No, just let it ring."

Chapter Four

Connor walked through the parking garage near his office building in downtown Tampa. He'd worked late and was on his way home to his wife. As he reached for the handle of his car door, a man stepped out from behind the support column beside him. Just then, he heard more footsteps close behind. A car passed the entrance. Its headlights reflected off the blade of a knife in the first man's hand. He looked at the man's face just before another from behind grabbed him. A third man spoke. "Hand over your wallet."

Connor forced himself awake. He could still see that man's face and the knife. The tap on his van window startled him. He sat up to see Jordan standing outside in a long flannel nightshirt. He checked his watch. It was only eleven thirty. He slid open the back door.

"Is everything okay?" he asked. "Has something happened to Lizzy?"

"Yes, everything's fine. Lizzy is sound asleep. I'm sorry if I woke you." She looked embarrassed. "I couldn't sleep. An old movie is coming on. I was thinking about making popcorn. Since it's Friday night and all, I thought you might like to join me. I'm sorry if I woke you. I'll go back inside and leave you alone."

"What's the movie?" Connor rubbed the sleep from his eyes.

"The Philadelphia Story. I don't know if you've ever seen it. You may not like it."

"Kate Hepburn, Cary Grant, I'm there. You do have butter for the popcorn, I hope."

"Of course I do. I even have Coke, beer, or Kool-Aid."

"What flavor of Kool-Aid?"

"Grape."

"I'll take the beer. Give me a minute to get dressed."

"Why? You're not naked."

"Did you come out here to see if I sleep naked?" he teased.

"No!"

Even in the moonlight, he saw her face redden. He stepped out of the van in a T-shirt and running shorts. Putting his arm around her shoulders, he walked toward the house.

"Come on, boss. I'll take you to the movies. I hear the girl at the concession stand is really cute."

They sat on either end of the sofa with a bowl of popcorn between them, sipping beer. Connor thoroughly enjoyed himself. He hadn't had a night like this in years. When the movie was over, he noticed that Jordan was squirming uncomfortably.

"Are you tired? I should let you get to bed."

"No. I can't sleep. I think I'll stay up and watch the next movie. You don't have to stay with me, though. I know you've worked hard today."

"That was yesterday. It's two o'clock now. What's the problem? Why are you wiggling so much?"

"No real problem. I think I must have pulled my back a little when we were moving furniture."

"Why didn't you say so? These magic fingers can fix anything." He ran up the stairs for just a minute and returned with the comforter and pillows from her bed. He spread the comforter on the floor in front of the television. "You're lucky this happened on a Cary Grant night. Lie on your stomach and put your arms up."

He rubbed her back trying to keep his mind on the movie. At the first commercial, he looked down to see that she had fallen asleep. He turned off the TV and lay down on the floor beside her. He just wanted to study her face for a moment before he left. He brought a lock of her hair to his face to breathe in its sweet scent. He placed a light kiss on his fingertips and touched her cheek. A soft feminine sigh slipped from her lips as she slept. Her steady breathing lulled him into a dreamless sleep almost instantly.

Sun was streaming through the window when Connor heard the voice of *Sponge Bob Square Pants*. Lizzy sat on the sofa watching the cartoon intently. Jordan had rolled over in the night. Her bottom nestled against his stomach. He felt her stir awake.

"What are you doing out of bed?" she asked sleepily.

"I'm waiting for my breakfast," Lizzy replied. "Are you two going to sleep all day?"

"What?" Jordan whipped her head around to find Connor beside her. Her eyes widened with panic. "No, no, I'm getting up now."

Connor grabbed her around the waist. "Don't get up, not yet," he whispered.

"Why, what's wrong?"

"If you get up, I'm going to be very embarrassed,

and you're going to have a lot of explaining to do." To his surprise, Jordan burst out laughing. He was not amused.

"Go upstairs and get dressed, Lizzy." When the coast was clear, Jordan sat up. "The bathroom is all yours, Romeo." She was still snickering as she skipped up the stairs.

****

Connor was nowhere in sight when Jordan and Lizzy returned to the living room.

"Help me get this stuff picked up before we cook breakfast." Jordan gathered the bedclothes from the floor.

"Maybe Connor will have breakfast with us today."

"I don't know. That's up to him."

"Is Connor my daddy now?" Lizzy asked.

"Why would you ask something like that?"

"My friend Ashley, in Tampa, says that mommies and daddies sleep together."

"We didn't sleep together. We just fell asleep in the same place. It was an accident."

"What's the difference?"

"Usually, mommies and daddies love each other," Jordan replied.

"Don't you love Connor?"

"Connor is just working here for a while." Jordan pulled her close. "After he's done, he'll be going away."

"I don't want him to go away. Why can't he stay here?" Lizzy cried.

The screen door in the kitchen slammed.

For the rest of the day, Connor stayed busy scraping loose paint from the outside of the house.

Jordan knew he'd overheard their conversation. She tried to think of what to say to him about it. She finally decided maybe it would be best to just ignore the whole incident. She waited for him to finish his shower.

"Dinner will be ready soon. You'd better hurry up. How do you feel about meatloaf tonight?" Her smile felt stiff.

"I'm not staying for dinner." He wouldn't look her in the eye. "I'll be back by Monday morning."

"My meatloaf isn't that bad."

"I need some time to myself." He walked away.

That night, Jordan tossed fitfully in her bed. At four in the morning she gave up the idea of sleeping and decided to make a pot of coffee. She sat at her kitchen table waiting for the coffeemaker to finish and picked up the kitten.

"I've been living alone for five years," she told Tom, stroking his soft head. "Why is my mind so unsettled now? Maybe it's just that I know Bobby Ray is going to be released soon. He'll be under the supervision of a parole officer, though. He wouldn't be allowed to follow me, even if he knew where I was. I need to get over this ridiculous paranoia."

A small, bright orange reflection spotted the side of her coffee carafe. She turned to look through the living room. Out the window were twin orange lights. A vehicle was parked in the driveway with only its parking beams on. Had Connor returned early? When she moved forward to get a better look, the glowing white headlights came on, blinding her momentarily. Then, the vehicle receded and moved down the road toward town.

"It was just the paper delivery," she assured Tom.

"I'm sure that's who it was, no doubt in my mind."

Now she was lying to the cat. She placed him on the floor and pulled a cookbook from the cabinet. By the time Lizzy woke, six pies lined the kitchen counter.

****

Connor sat on the bank of the creek. He'd been so deep in thought he'd forgotten to throw his line in the water for over an hour.

Lizzy was just a little girl. She hadn't meant for her words to hurt him the way they had. She didn't know how much he ached to have a family of his own. How could she? He hadn't even realized it until lately. What hurt more was Jordan's complete dismissal of the idea.

What did he expect her to say? It must have been shocking for her to wake up next to him. His own wife hadn't lost any time filing for divorce after she'd seen what had been done to him.

He'd signed the papers in his hospital bed, letting her have almost everything. He'd given up his career and walked away from his whole life. He'd never looked back. Since then, he hadn't wanted another woman for more than a couple of hours. He'd found a few willing to leave a bar with him. It didn't happen often, and they weren't the most reputable ladies in town.

Jordan was different though. She was clean, fresh, and beautiful. She was so expressive; he knew she would be a bottomless well of passion. She was the kind of woman made for a man's arms. So why was she alone?

Connor jumped to his feet when the bushes rustled behind him.

"I see you've found my favorite hiding place."

Arnold Coleman walked toward the water.

"I don't see a fishing pole in your hand, old man."

"Sometimes I just like to watch the water." Without turning he asked, "How's the job going?"

"I've got a good start on it. It's a very nice house."

"I know. Elizabeth Holbrook was a close friend. I went over every Sunday evening to have a glass of tea and a talk out on that front porch. It was on one of those evenings that she had her stroke. I had to be the one to call Jordan four years ago and have her take Elizabeth away. I miss that front porch." He sat on a tree stump. They both looked out on the water.

"Lizzy must have been named after her."

"Yep, Elizabeth, Elizabeth Holbrook," Arnold confirmed. "She's like her too, smart as a whip. Her looks are different though. Elizabeth was a small woman with light blonde hair and the bluest eyes you've ever seen. Jordan must have taken after her daddy, whoever he was."

Connor raised a brow, but let it pass.

"Why doesn't Lizzy have her daddy's name?"

"That man was incarcerated just before she was born. What a piece of work he was. Jordan gave the baby her maiden name and took it back herself, once she was divorced."

"How would Jordan get mixed up with a criminal? She doesn't seem the type."

"She's not the type, but we all make mistakes." Arnold picked up a long twig and began breaking it into little pieces. "Butler came to work for the company Jordan worked for in Tampa. He said he was an orphan. He claimed to be in trouble for stealing as a kid, in order to feed himself. Butler also admitted he'd been in jail later for beating a man half to death because the guy had attacked him in an alley. Jordan felt sorry for him, which is what he'd intended.

He'd been in jail all right, but he'd been guilty. By the time Jordan found out the truth, she was married and pregnant. Butler beat her up the first time when he found out she was having the baby. Jordan knew he was still at his old tricks. The people he brought home were that sort too. She didn't know what to do. One day they were at one of those little quickie stores. Butler decided to hold the place up."

"You mean, while she was with him?" Connor asked in disbelief.

"He used her as a hostage. Holding a knife on a pregnant woman will usually make a man open a cash register pretty fast. The videotape was very clear. You could see every bruise on her face. I think the jury would have convicted on that alone. Since then it's just been her and Lizzy. I'm surprised to hear that she lets you in the house. She doesn't usually trust anybody these days. I just hope he never finds her."

"Why? He can't hold her responsible for what he did."

"Oh yes he can. He can hold her responsible for getting him caught, too."

"You said the police had a clear videotape."

"But they didn't have his name and location until Jordan called and turned him in."

"Damn," Connor snapped. No wonder she had the attitude. "How did you find out about all of this?"

"Elizabeth. She was in that courtroom every day. She was furious when he was only sentenced for ten to fifteen years."

"You two must have been close."

"Not as close as I would have liked." Arnold tossed the rest of the twig into the water and stood. "I gave her too much space. I lost my chance."

Arnold had almost reached the edge of the woods when Connor called out to him.

"Hey Coleman, how long did you say his sentence was?"

"Ten to fifteen."

"How long ago was that?"

"About five and a half years…right before Lizzy was born."

Connor decided to pack up his van and head back early. He had a few things to look into.

Chapter Five

The stubby pencil broke in Bobby Ray's hand. Damn. He wouldn't be able to finish the picture until after his next trip to the commissary. It was bad enough they were the size of the pencils you'd find in a bowling alley or miniature golf course. The only way he had to sharpen them was to use his teeth. But, this one was already too small.

Thinking about Jordan always put him in a foul mood. Not only was his being here her fault but he hadn't heard a word from her in all this time.

His lawyer had promised that if he signed the divorce papers she'd sent, his chance of parole would be better. At least that had been true, but it still took too long. That same day, his lawyer had also told him that she had given birth to a girl. She couldn't even give him a son. She never did anything right. To hear she'd named the brat after her grandmother had been the last insult. He pictured the old lady's face glaring at him from across the courtroom, so high and mighty. That was okay. He had a plan.

He'd met Bennett in the chow hall last February and they'd become friends before Bennett was released. It was convenient to have a lawyer as a friend, even if the guy was a weasel. He was collecting information for him right this minute.

Bobby Ray swore he'd have his revenge, come hell

or high water.

****

As soon as Connor pulled in behind the barn, Jordan raced toward the van. Her thick braid bounced against her back and her long legs stroked the air like a gazelle. He was relieved to see a wide smile on her face.

"Connor, I'm so glad you're back. I've been about to bust waiting to tell somebody my great news."

"What's up, boss?" he asked.

"I've got a job," she squealed. "I went to Holly's with a pie for the barbecue. Hey, do you want some pie?"

"Maybe later, get back to your story. You got a job making pies?"

"No silly, at the bank."

"You took pies to the bank?"

"No, listen carefully. You're getting this all mixed up."

Connor burst out laughing. He loved this woman. Oh my God! He loved this woman! How had that happened?

"Start from the beginning and stick to the story. I think we can get through this before morning."

"Okay, listen. I took a pie to Holly's house. Her husband is the bank manager at the Merchants Bank. He needs a new teller. That's me." Jordan jumped up and down clapping. She didn't look any older than Lizzy right then and she was adorable. "The lady who runs the daycare Holly's boys go to, Mrs. Rogers on First Street, says they'll take Lizzy. Isn't that great?"

"Yes, it's great. My boss has a job. Do I get a raise and what kind of pie do you have?"

She looked up at him sheepishly, "I have two apples and two peaches left."

"I leave for one day and you start binge baking? Anyone else would think that you missed me." He grinned.

"Did you eat? Are you hungry?"

"Do you have any of that meatloaf left?"

"Cold meatloaf sandwiches, yum! I haven't eaten either."

He threw his arm around her shoulders as they started toward the house, and then stopped.

"Maybe I should take a shower first."

"Maybe you should," she said with her nose crinkled. He grabbed her into a bear hug as she squirmed and gasped with laughter. "Now I'll need a shower too."

"I'm always willing to share."

"Dream on, Romeo."

****

Jordan's first week at her new job was fabulous. She met old friends and made new ones. The work was easy to learn. Each day she came home to a new room. Connor did all the decorating and his taste was incredible. On Monday, her living room was painted warm gold. He'd put in the faux Persian rug, green leather furniture, throw pillows and candles for accent. Tuesday, her dining room was the same gold with a plum table runner and a floral arrangement that looked great with her grandmother's china. Wednesday he added decorative tile at the back of the kitchen counters. He also installed a large island in the middle of the floor with a pot rack over the top. Thursday, the bathroom became a rich cream color with matching tile.

The new towels and rugs were burgundy and gold. Friday, the spare bedroom had cream walls with burgundy striped drapes and comforter. Every evening a hot meal was waiting. Even better than all that, the phone calls had stopped.

"Connor, you'll make someone a great wife someday," she jokingly remarked after supper. "The house is beautiful and your cooking is better than mine. You're spoiling us.

"Now that the downstairs is finished, what are you going to do next?"

"If you're up for shopping tomorrow afternoon, I could get started on the upstairs."

"We only have three rooms up there." The realization of how fast the work was getting done made her sad, but she couldn't keep him here forever.

"I have to get back to the outside sooner or later."

"I guess we could start tomorrow." Getting it over with would probably be best, for her as well as Lizzy.

"The security system is being installed in the morning. It's state of the art with a battery backup. It covers all the doors and windows upstairs and down. They monitor for fires and break-ins. It even has a panic button for medical emergencies and whatever."

"Lizzy, it's time for you to go upstairs and get ready for your bath," Jordan said, frowning. After Lizzy flitted from the room, she turned back to Connor. "I don't remember paying for a security system. I hadn't even made up my mind yet about having one."

"I've got some money put back. It's a gift. You can pay the monthly service fee. I got you a good deal," he replied, lightly.

"What makes you think I need it?"

"Don't argue with me about this." His tone reminded Jordan of her old life. It made the food she'd just eaten feel like a rock in her stomach. "And don't pull that boss card out either. We both know why you need it. Mr. Coleman told me about your ex-husband. I looked into it. I know he's getting out of prison at the end of the month. Do you realize how soon that is? It's less than a week away."

"You had no right digging into my business." If she didn't assert her independence now, she never would.

"I had every right." He rubbed his hands over his face, before he went on. "You and Lizzy have become very important to me. I couldn't live with myself if anything happened to you. I have to do all I can to protect you. Why are you so against protecting yourself? Do you plan on being a victim for the rest of your life?"

How dare he take control that way? This was her home, her family, and her life.

"Look who's talking. You hide yourself away in a beat-up old van. Do you ever plan to return to the real world? What are you so afraid of?"

"I'm not afraid of the world, it's afraid of me. There's no way to hide these scars." He tilted his face up and to the side to make his point. "Have you seen the looks I get when I'm in town? Pay attention some time. People look at me with disgust or revulsion. I've heard kids ask their moms if I'm a monster. Even after people get used to me, they look at me with pity. Can you honestly say it wasn't the first thing you saw when we met?"

"Of course I noticed. I felt bad because of how

much it must have hurt. Don't you realize that people look at you the way they do because they see themselves in your place? If they saw you the way Lizzy and I do, smiling and happy, they'd get past it. But you don't give people a chance."

"How did this get turned around to me?" Connor threw his napkin onto the table. "I'm going to bed. I'll be here to watch the security people when they get here in the morning. That system will be installed and you will use it." He stormed out of the house with Jordan close behind him. He turned around halfway to his van and she almost ran into him. "What?" he yelled at her.

"We just had our first fight and I don't feel like it's over," she yelled back.

"So what do you want now? Are we supposed to kiss and make up or something?" he sneered.

"Well, as they say, never go to bed mad." She threw her arms around his neck and kissed him hard on the lips. It was the first time she'd kissed a man in more than five years, but it had never felt this good.

"I don't know who they are," he said breathlessly, "but I like them."

"Okay, well, goodnight, Connor."

"Good night, boss."

They turned in separate directions and walked away.

****

The next morning the security system was hooked up. The installers instructed Jordan in how to use it. They even showed Lizzy how to find the panic button. Then Connor went over the instructions with them twice more. Finally, Jordan threw her hands into the air and walked away.

"Can I take a nap now?" Lizzy asked. "This whole thing has worn me out."

While she slept, Connor and Jordan went through the upstairs rooms to decide what had to be replaced. A couple of boxes sat in the hallway, outside Jordan's room.

"What's all this?"

"I need to get those up to the attic. It's just stuff I brought from Tampa, Lizzy's baby clothes and toys, old photo albums. Things like that."

"Well, there's no time like the present." Connor hefted the biggest box to his shoulder. "Open the attic and I'll take them up."

Jordan pulled the rope letting down the steps and Connor carried the first box up without incident. When he lifted the second box, the bottom let go. Pictures and photo albums scattered over the floor. He set the box down to scoop the loose photos together. There were pictures of Jordan throughout her school years and baby pictures of Lizzy. A lot of people he didn't know…except one.

The face of the man from his dream lay in the middle of the pile. The face smiling up at him had the same sneer as it did that night in the parking garage. He fell back against the wall and slid down. He sat with his knees up and head down drawing large amounts of air through his nose and blowing it out. Jordan ran to soak a washcloth for his face. Before she could finish he was leaning over the toilet beside her, his stomach heaving as it emptied.

"What happened? Is it the heat?" She wiped his pale face.

"I need to lie down for a while. I need to get out to

my van."

"You're not going anywhere. You're staying in this house until I know you're okay."

"I'm not sick, I just…why do you have a picture of that man?"

"I don't know what you're talking about. I have a lot of pictures."

While she was in her room turning down the bed he returned to the hall and found the picture he'd dropped. He held it out to her when she came back.

"I forgot I had that," she whispered. "I'd rather not talk about it."

"Who is he, Jordan?"

It was the first time he'd called her by her first name. He tried to keep his voice even and calm.

"That's my ex-husband, Bobby Ray Butler. I don't understand." She took the picture from his hand holding it by its edge as though it were covered in something vile. "Get some rest. We can talk later."

Connor lay with his back to the window. He couldn't stand the sunlight right now. His stomach and head hurt. His heart was breaking. Lizzy's father, Jordan's former husband and lover, this couldn't be happening. He wanted to scream. He wanted to cry. He wanted to rip the man's heart out and feed it to him.

His attackers had never been identified. He had never had the satisfaction of justice. He would never have justice now. Even if he could prove this was the man who had used that knife on him, even if he watched him fry in an electric chair for the crime, he had stolen something much more precious from him now. He'd stolen the first dream that Connor had allowed himself to have in six years.

Could he look at Lizzy and not see that man somewhere in her little face? Could he look at Jordan and not picture his hands on her body? Connor wished he had died that night in the parking garage. He wished he could close his eyes and never wake up. All the visions, past, present, and imagined ran through his head. His brain couldn't function any more. He fell asleep with tears of anger on his cheeks.

Chapter Six

Jordan went through the afternoon on autopilot, but her nerves were wearing thin. Finally, she decided to make a call.

"Hey, Holly, I hate to ask, but could you do me a favor?"

"Sure, girl, I'd do anything for you." There was a pause. "You don't sound so good. What's the matter?"

"I'm under the weather today. I don't think I can handle Lizzy tonight. She's been getting along with the boys so well, I was wondering…"

"Don't even ask. She's welcome here anytime. I've always wanted to spend the evening baking cookies with a little girl in my kitchen. All my boys care about is eating them. Can I polish her little fingernails?"

"She'd love it." Jordan was thankful to have such an understanding friend. "I'm really sorry to impose like this."

"Don't give it another thought. Just see if you can get a pair of pajamas packed before I get there. Then, you can climb into bed and get to feeling better. Do you need me to pick anything up for you on my way over?"

"No, I'm sure I'll be fine by tomorrow. You're always such a lifesaver, Holly. Thank you."

"Just get yourself better darlin'. I'll be there in fifteen minutes."

Lizzy was excited about her sleepover. She waved

out the car window as they pulled away. This was the first time they wouldn't be sleeping under the same roof. It felt strange.

Jordan sat on the front porch and finally allowed herself to think about the incident with Connor. There was only one thing she could think of that would cause him to have such a strong reaction to Bobby Ray's picture. Guilt coursed through her body. Maybe if she'd found a way to stop Bobby Ray sooner Connor would be a happy, successful man today. He'd have a home, a family and friends. He wouldn't feel the need to hide from the world.

What must he think of her? She had been married to a violent animal, had his child. Everything he'd done to her couldn't compare to what Connor had been through. How many other people's lives had her ex-husband ruined?

The setting sun shined on her like a spotlight. She suddenly felt exposed. She went into the living room and just sat, numbness inching through her limbs and into her body. She watched the sun disappear, leaving her in total darkness. She closed her eyes.

****

Connor found Jordan sleeping in a living room chair. It didn't seem right to just walk past her. Not after he'd spent the last two hours sleeping in her bed. But what could he say to explain how he'd reacted to the picture? He didn't have a chance to figure it out before her eyes blinked open.

"Are you absolutely sure?" she murmured. "Are you positive it was him?"

"It was him." How could she be so perceptive?

A tear streaked down each cheek before she had a

chance to turn her back. Her sobs tore at his heart. Suddenly she jumped from the chair and ran toward the stairs. He couldn't leave her like this. When he caught up to her he grabbed her shoulders and pulled her against his chest. He rocked her in his arms until she regained some composure.

"Did you love him?"

"I thought I did, a long time ago. That didn't last long." Jordan sniffed and wiped her eyes. "He was an animal. All he cared about was taking whatever he wanted and destroying everything else. I got the worst of both. When he was mad, it was really bad. When he was happy, it was even worse."

She couldn't look him in the eye. He understood what she was saying and it made his skin crawl. He hated this guy worse now than he had six years ago. What kind of hell had the man put Jordan through?

He lowered himself onto the sofa with her in his arms. They clung to each other for several minutes.

"God, what a pair we are," he scoffed. "Both of us were victims of the same monster."

"When were you in Tampa?" she asked. Bobby Ray had never gone far from the area.

"I was born and raised in Tampa. My parents and brother still live there." He knew she really wanted to know when he'd been attacked. He ran his finger down the scar on his cheek. "This happened six years ago. They didn't try to make it pretty, because they didn't think I'd live. I was in a coma when they found me. They thought I'd probably suffered extensive brain damage from the beating. I have more scars."

"I know," she admitted. "I saw you out the window the second day you were here. Can you tell me what happened?"

It took him a minute to gather it all in his mind. Then he told her everything he could remember. Sitting in the dark in each other's arms made it easier.

"I'm glad your family was there to support you," she said when he'd finished.

"I suppose it helped, but it was hard. My mother couldn't stop crying. My father and brother were angry and frustrated that they couldn't do anything about it. My wife visited once. Divorce papers were in my hand within a month. She said she was sorry, but she just couldn't live with it." He pointed to his left cheek.

"I didn't know you'd been married. Do you have children?"

"No, she didn't want any. When I was young and arrogant I didn't think I did either. Now that the chance has passed, I do want them, badly. Isn't that ironic? I guess you always want what you can't have."

"Why can't you have children?" Her brows knitted in concern.

"Look at this face. Do you think any woman would want to walk down the aisle with me? Besides that, I'd probably scare a poor baby to death. I'm getting too old anyway."

"You are so full of shit. You can't be over thirty-five. That's not too old. And for your information, babies don't judge. They don't have any frame of reference. And tons of women would have you. You're smart, kind, funny, and you have an awesome body."

"Have you been peeking?"

It felt good to laugh again. Jordan started to stand, but Connor tugged her back into his lap.

"Where's Lizzy?" he asked softly.

"She's spending the night with the Douglases." Her voice was low and her eyes watched his lips.

He pulled her face down to his. He hesitated and Jordan leaned in to meet him halfway. Her kiss was the sweetest he'd ever known. When he pulled back, her hands were splayed across his chest. His heart beating strong and fast under her palm. His erection throbbed insistently against her leg. He leaned his forehead to hers, savoring their closeness. She stroked his left cheek, just once before he grabbed her wrist.

"Does it hurt?" she asked.

"No."

"I want to touch every inch of you." She stood and led him to the spare bedroom.

Moonlight was spreading a soft blue glow over the room. Connor walked to the window to close the drapes.

"Please don't do that," Jordan said. "I want to see you. I want to know that you're the man in my bed tonight. I don't want to think of anyone or anything else."

"Are you sure about this, Jordan?" Connor stood with his head down, gathering his courage.

"I'm willing to beg, if that's what it takes. I've never wanted anything more."

He turned just as she dropped her shirt on the chair arm with her jeans. There she stood in a peach colored lace bra and panty set. She was tall, strong, and proud. Her thick copper braid hung over her shoulder to the bottom of one beautiful breast. A moan escaped his throat. He crossed to her in two long strides. His kiss was more urgent and passionate. His hands skimmed down the sides of her back to her hips. Her hands slid

under his T-shirt pushing it past his chest. She pulled
back long enough to draw the shirt over his head. Her
skin against his felt like silk. While he was with her,
she'd never have to beg for anything.

Jordan backed him to the edge of the bed. He
unfastened her bra and let it fall to the floor. He
lowered her panties slowly, amazed at the length of her
smooth, shapely legs. A tiny shiver ran through her as
his lips and tongue tasted every inch of her body. Her
scent was like freshly washed sheets and sweet
honeysuckle.

Jordan pushed against his shoulders until he lay on
his back. Leaning over, she kissed him with all the
passion he had imagined she'd have. Her kisses made a
path down his neck and chest to his stomach. His
muscles contracted when she ran her tongue across the
scars there. She tugged the snap at the top of his jeans
and the zipper slid open. She eased them over his legs
as she continued her exploration.

He sat up to look her in the eyes. "You can change
your mind anytime you want. I wouldn't blame you."

"I need you. Please don't pull back from me now."
Desperation clouded her expression as she looked down
over his naked body. "It occurs to me that maybe this
isn't what you want. I didn't really give you a choice.
That was selfish of me, I'm sorry."

Connor got up to kneel on the bed facing her. "I
can't put into words how much I want you. I've wanted
you since that first morning we met. You're so beautiful
and vibrant. You make my blood race and my heart
pound. You drive me crazy. I just don't understand why
you want me."

"You take my craziness away." She shrugged.

"You make me feel calm and safe. You seriously listen to me and value my opinions. You appreciate the things I do. You make me feel normal." She giggled as he leaned over to kiss her again. "Besides that, you're absolutely hot. The scars make you look incredibly rugged."

He reached up to pull the band from the end of her braid. He gathered his own hair into a low ponytail and used the band to hold it back.

"Enough talk," he growled. "You've convinced me."

As he leaned over her, she wrapped her legs around him, welcoming him into her body, into heaven. He'd always loved the warm silky feel of a woman, but Jordan was like no other he'd ever known. Her liquid movements, soft sounds, and exquisite expression of desire nearly undid him, but his need to please her was stronger. The long awaited sensations were so intense that neither lasted. She shuddered to an orgasm and he quickly followed, thankful that the night had just begun.

Connor woke the next morning with Jordan flicking the tip of her tongue behind his left ear. He rolled onto his back, groaned and stretched. It felt good to lay naked in a real bed, a warm woman's body pressed against him. She quickly sat up tucking her legs under her and laughed.

"It's time to get up, Romeo. Lizzy could be home any minute. It's almost eight o'clock."

He rubbed his eyes with the palms of his hands before opening them on her. She sat in the middle of the bed totally naked and unashamed. This was his first clear look at her in the light of day. Her braid had come loose and left her hair falling in tangles down her back.

You could clearly see where a bikini had shielded her most tender areas. Her breasts were large and round with high pink nipples. Her bellybutton was small in her soft flat stomach. No one would guess that she was the mother of a five-year-old. The triangle below was the same dark auburn as the rest of her hair. She had legs that went on forever. If he didn't get out of the bed, they'd be there when Lizzy came home.

"Is the coffee ready, boss?"

"It will be by the time you get the newspaper."

Connor grabbed a clean pair of shorts off the dryer and stepped into them. He pulled his T-shirt over his head as he walked out to the mailbox for the Sunday paper. As he was reading the front-page a car pulled into the driveway beside him. It had barely come to a stop when Lizzy leaped out of the back seat and into his arms.

"I had the best time ever! Look at my fingernails!" She held them up for him to admire. "They're pink now."

A short shapely woman with a friendly smile stepped out of the passenger seat and held out her hand to him. "Hi! I'm Holly Douglas, Jordan's friend. You must be the Connor I've heard so much about."

Connor was speechless as he shook her hand. She looked him straight in the eye without flinching.

"Holly!" Jordan stepped out on the porch wrapped in her bathrobe. "You brought Charlie and the boys with you! Come on in for some coffee."

"Just one cup, sweetie. We only stopped by to let Lizzy get dressed. She wants to go to church with us. We had a blast last night with her. I hate to give her back." Holly grinned. "I'm glad to see you're feeling better."

A man came from the other side of car. "I could sure use another cup of coffee. Maybe it'll help keep me awake during the service." He held his hand out to Connor. His left arm was missing. "Nice to meet you Connor, I'm Holly's slave, Charlie."

"Nice to meet you too."

Lizzy looked from Connor to her mother and back again. "Did you two accidentally fall asleep in the same place again?"

Even though Holly and Charlie found her question amusing, Jordan and Connor were mortified.

Chapter Seven

"What'cha got there?"

Bobby Ray looked up to see Bennett's friend, Doris Pritchett, approaching. He folded the small notebook closed and placed it, and his new pencil in the pocket of his shirt. She was the last person he'd share his art with. He suspiciously surveyed the visiting area for anyone listening.

"Has Bennett found out anything yet?"

The middle-aged, bleached blonde sat on the opposite side of the picnic table. She lit a cigarette. He could tell by the heavy mascara flaking under her eyes that she had been working all night on a street corner downtown. Her hands shook from the need for her current drug of choice.

"She's in a small town down south called Mayville," Doris informed him. "She works at the Mayville Merchants Bank as a teller.

"Word is, she just inherited a house and a sizeable bank account from her granny." Doris took another long draw from her cigarette and coughed. "We're lucky she was named in her granny's obituary or Bennett never would have found her. All he had to do was put her name on the internet thingy.

A waitress at the diner there was a big help too. The people in that place love flapping their gums about other people's business.

"Bennett said he's been following her all over town and she's never caught on. What an idiot. She thinks she's all safe and cozy there. Or at least she did before he made a couple of anonymous calls to her house. Hell, he even knows where the kid stays during the day."

"Is he having any trouble with the paperwork we talked about?"

"He says it's been a piece of cake. She should be getting it soon." She threw the cigarette butt on the ground and twisted her dirty sandal over it. "I'll be here on Wednesday to pick you up. It'll take at least a week to get this thing going. You're welcome to stay at my place if you want."

"Thanks, Doris. I'll think it over." He suppressed a cringe. God only knew how many diseases she carried. She probably lived in a crack house. He wouldn't need her after Wednesday afternoon.

****

Jordan sat with Connor on the porch while Lizzy took her afternoon nap. They were silent for a long time, lost in their own thoughts until it became awkward.

"I really liked your friends," Connor blurted. "How did you meet Holly? She seems so much different than you."

"We were a couple of misfits in school." Jordan looked out over her freshly cut lawn and reminisced. "I guess that's what brought us together. We were in second grade when I moved here. Holly has always been a little overweight. You know how kids are. They teased her something awful. I was the new kid. They just didn't have much to do with me. Later on, we hung out when the other kids were having parties and dates. You know how it is."

"You must have gotten to know the other kids after a while. Why weren't you out on dates too?"

"I didn't usually get asked." She smiled. "I was a whole head taller than most of the boys and had a face full of freckles. My nickname in school was Spot."

"If they could only see you now." Connor cupped her chin and brought her face to meet his. "You sure outgrew your awkwardness."

"Are you kidding? It's even worse now." Jordan pulled away. "I'm taller than most of the men I know. My hair is a mass of curls and I still have the freckles. Everything on my body is starting to slide south. I have a huge butt and stretch marks. Everything a man looks for in a woman, right?"

"I didn't notice any of those things." He frowned as he tugged her face back around. "Well, I did see the freckles and they're absolutely fantastic. And, if you're really worried about your hair, I met someone the other day that can help you out. But please don't cut it all off. I think you're beautiful. I have since the minute I first saw you. I just can't believe you'd ever have anything to do with somebody like me."

"Connor, there's something I think we need to talk about." Jordan looked down to avoid his gaze. "Now that Lizzy is home, well, I don't want her to get confused or get the wrong idea about things. She seems to be more observant than I expected. Or, maybe we're just too obvious."

"You don't have to say it. I understand. I don't know if it's such a good idea either. I'll be leaving in a few weeks and it's not going to be easy for me as it is.

I've gotten pretty attached to both of you. But you came here to start a new life. I know I'm not part of those plans. There's no need for me to make your life any more complicated than it is already."

Jordan couldn't look at him. She was overcome by sadness. "You're a truly wonderful person." The statement didn't seem like enough. She wanted to wrap her arms around him and tell him he was the most amazing man she'd ever met. She wanted to tell him that last night had been the most fantastic night of her life. But she couldn't. He was right. It would only complicate things.

"You know it's Sunday and I don't have a single thing to do," Connor declared. "We haven't really taken advantage of this beautiful weather, or this new landscaping. Why don't you put together something simple for dinner and we can have a picnic right out here on the lawn."

"That's not a bad idea. Lizzy would love it." She sprang from her chair, and then paused. "You know, I've been meaning to get my old bike out of the barn. It's just Lizzy's size and it's in pretty good shape. A little oil and air in the tires and I bet she could learn to ride it."

"I'll get right on it, boss."

They spent the rest of the evening playing with Lizzy. They ate fried chicken and potato salad on a blanket in the back yard. Music played from Connor's van, parked a few yards away. Lizzy wobbled up and down the driveway on the old bicycle with Connor holding on to the back of the seat. They'd found an old basketball that he taught Lizzy to toss into an empty box while her kitten, Tom, chased grasshoppers.

"If Lizzy grows up to be like her mother, she may have a future with the NBA," he teased.

She and Connor didn't speak on a personal level, but they stole glances at each other all evening.

"I'd better get these dishes and leftovers inside while there's still enough light to find them." Inside Jordan put away the food and ran dishwater. She was washing dishes at the sink when a pretty song drifted through the window. It was a lullaby that played on and on. She had never heard it before, and it was lovely. Jordan wiped her hands and went back out.

There was enough twilight to see Connor sitting in the middle of the blanket with Lizzy in his lap, a guitar lying across their legs. The song abruptly stopped.

"You have a beautiful voice."

"I do okay." He laid the guitar aside and picked up Lizzy. She had almost fallen asleep.

"I don't think I've ever heard that song before."

"It's a song my mother always sang to us." His smile seemed sad. "I think she always wished she'd had a little girl. She used to sing it to my brother and me sometimes, though, and I guess it just stuck."

"Do you ever see your family?"

"No." His smile faded.

"I can tell you miss them."

"Every day." He carried Lizzy inside without another word.

After Lizzy had been bathed and put to bed, Jordan went back to the kitchen for a cup of coffee. Connor's song was still playing in her head. Looking out the window, she saw the bicycle lying by the driveway. She thought about how nice the evening had been. She decided to take the bike back to the barn in case it rained during the night. A light sprinkle tapped her head on the way.

Jordan had walked halfway through the barn when something shuffled to her right. She suddenly realized she was alone in the dark. An image of Bobby Ray flashed through her mind. She screamed and jumped to her left, falling over a sawhorse.

"I'm sorry I scared you. Are you okay? I should have said something. I'm so sorry." Connor helped her back to her feet.

Jordan stood for a moment catching her breath. Her heart was pounding like a jackhammer. Her hands braced against his chest. "Oh God, I can't believe how stupid I am. I thought you were him. You scared me to death."

"You see why I worry about you? You're not prepared. You should be in the house with that damn alarm on." He was clearly annoyed.

"Don't you think I know what an idiot I am? I married that monster. I deserve what I get, but where does that leave Lizzy? I'm not saying you're wrong. I just don't know what to do about it. I can't live like this for the rest of my life, not knowing when he's going to show up, or what he's going to do. I feel like I'm losing my mind. The last thing I need is you reminding me. What are you doing out here anyway?"

"I was just wandering around thinking," he said more quietly. "There's something I want to tell you. I want you to know that last night meant a lot to me. I had forgotten what it felt like to be that close to someone. There have been other women since...my divorce. But, it was just sex. You were so much more than that. I just wanted you to know. I wanted to say thank you for making me feel normal again."

"You are normal. After last night, I can't say you're average. That would be a huge understatement. But there isn't anything wrong with you. As I see it, you're pretty awesome. You took me, a neurotic Amazon woman, and made me feel desirable. That's what I call a miracle."

"You are desirable. You are downright amazing. And you are not an idiot. You don't deserve any of this. You deserve a man who can love and protect you from that psycho. For now, you'll have to settle for me. Even if I do have to stay away from you, I intend to see you and Lizzy through this." He ran a finger through a lock of hair that had escaped her braid and then held her hand as he led her back to the house. He lifted her fingers to his lips before he left her at the door.

Jordan watched him walk back to his van. She was fascinated by the way he moved. He seemed half man, half panther. All his sleek muscles moved in a graceful rhythm. He had been hers for one night. If she had known the effect that one night would have on her, she probably wouldn't have done it. She didn't regret it though. And, she would never forget it.

Chapter Eight

For the next week, Connor made their routine appear as normal as possible. Jordan didn't need to know that he was taking small steps back into his old life.

Every evening, she came home to a clean house and a home cooked meal. He had used the accounts she had opened in town to continue the redecorating. On Monday, the upstairs bathroom had been painted pale yellow. The silk floral arrangement on the white counter matched the red and blue towels. A painting of a mother and daughter walking through a brightly colored garden dominated the room. On Tuesday, Lizzy's bedroom was the same pale yellow with new white furniture and brightly colored accents. He had used an old quilt Jordan had as a child to cover the bed. The flowers stenciled at the tops of the walls had ladybugs, butterflies, dragonflies and fairies. In the corner was a small table and chairs. Her books had been neatly lined on shelves. Lizzy swore she would keep her new room neat as she hugged and kissed every inch of Connor's face.

On Wednesday, Jordan's room became a pale, sage green. The four-poster bed and heavy oak furniture remained, but a bistro table and two chairs had been added in front of the window. The comforter and drapes were dark gold satin with tiny red flowers embroidered around the edges. The chairs and bed were accented with red and green satin throw pillows. Candles had been placed in clusters throughout the room. It was a romantic setting for two. Connor stayed in the doorway to watch her reaction.

"This is magnificent. I don't feel like it's mine."

"You're magnificent," he replied. "This was the hardest room for me to decorate. Nothing seemed to match your beauty. That's why I saved it for last. I'm glad you like it. It took me so long I didn't have time to finish. Close your eyes and count to fifty. Then, the inside of the house will be done."

As she counted, Connor slid the picture out from under her bed. He hit the nail on the hallway wall twice to place it in the perfect spot, and then returned to tap her shoulder.

"I'd better get downstairs before my roast burns." He waited at the bottom of the stairs for a moment to, once again, see her reaction. As she walked out of her room she found the picture of her grandparents, restored, enlarged, and framed. He could tell by her gasp that she loved it.

A few minutes later, Jordan joined him in the kitchen wiping tears from her eyes. Connor took her into his arms and just held her.

"What's wrong Jordan? You've hardly said a word since you got home. Now, you're crying. Did you have a bad day at work or is it something I've done? You know I can change anything you don't like. Just talk to me, sweetheart. I can't stand to see you cry."

She whispered into his chest, "Everything you've done has made my life more beautiful. I'm just afraid that it's going to come crashing down on me. Do you know what today is?"

"I know. It's the first of the month. I've had it on my mind all day too. We're not going to borrow trouble though." He used a finger to tilt her face up to his. "Whatever happens, we'll face it together. He'll be back behind bars before you know it. He can't help it. Until then, I'm going to be watching. Now let's call Lizzy down and have a nice dinner."

He and Jordan were quiet while Lizzy chattered on about her day at Mrs. Rogers's daycare. They replied when necessary and glanced at each other often. There was no doubt what was on Jordan's mind. Bobby Ray Butler was a free man.

"We've got plans to make."

"What do you mean? What plans?" Jordan inquired.

"Saturday is Heritage Day. We should do something to celebrate. We need some fun and fireworks. I bet they've got some kind of shindig planned in town."

"What's that?" Lizzy asked.

"It's like a party or celebration. Wouldn't you like to go to a party?" he answered.

Lizzy squealed and bounced in her chair as Jordan's eyes went wide and her face went white. "I don't know if that's a good idea. Do you think it's safe to go out like that?"

"Do you plan to stay in the house for the rest of your life? Are you going to give someone that kind of power over you? I've done that for years now, and I don't plan to do it any longer. I would never let anything happen to either of you, not ever."

****

Bobby Ray wiped the blood off his hands with a rag in the floorboard of the car. He'd have to find a drugstore to get some alcohol. Why wouldn't the bitch just leave him alone? He'd had to fight like hell to avoid STDs in prison. He sure as hell wasn't letting that shit-bag give him one on the first day he got out.

After leaving the state prison, Doris had driven the car down a dirt road into the country.

"Where the hell are we going? This isn't the way to Gainesville. I need to get my hands on a car before the end of the day. I don't have time for side trips."

"I've got something for you, baby. I know you've been waiting a long time." Doris had stepped out of the car to pull off her sweat-stained tank top. All he could see were ribs sticking out from her tight skin. Next, the stretchy, short skirt came off. She was disgusting to look at.

"Do you actually expect to do this here, on the side of the road?" he'd asked.

"We could find a nice place in the trees."

"Yeah, let's do that. I'll show you a good time, honey." He kicked her discarded clothes under the car before he followed. She didn't know he'd removed his belt until it was coming over her head to circle her throat. Even after she had stopped kicking, he wasn't sure she was dead. He picked up a large rock to pound her head, over and over. When his arms were tired, he looked down and saw the blood on his shirt. He quickly tore it off and threw it aside, glad he'd worn an undershirt.

The girly keychain hanging from the steering column brought his thoughts back to the present. He yanked the stupid pink furry ball from the ring and threw it over his shoulder.

He'd never killed anybody before. No one he'd actually watched die anyway. It had been so cool. If there is one thing he'd learned from his long stint in prison, it was not to leave witnesses.

Nobody would miss an old junkie hooker. By the time anybody found her body in these woods she wouldn't be recognizable. Too bad she was only carrying two hundred bucks. He had to get his hands on more money. At least the bitch's old car would get him down south. He just had to be careful not to get pulled over. Maybe Bennett could help him get a driver's license. Maybe even a new name.

On the way, he'd find him a pretty, young girl to release some of his tension. He wanted to be in top condition when he got to Jordan. She may not be much to look at, but she was a damn good fuck. Too bad she never liked it much. She probably hadn't had any since he'd been gone, the frigid bitch.

Bobby Ray drove the seven hours to Ft. Myers. Off the interstate, he found a cheap hotel in a small town. He needed to sleep, take a hot shower, eat a decent meal, and find a woman.

He slept for ten hours in a king-sized bed. He couldn't remember the last time he'd been able to lie on his back and stretch out in any direction he wanted. Then he took a long hot shower in total privacy. He used every soft, white towel in the room before putting his one set of clothes back on. Traces of Doris's blood were splattered on his shoes and pant legs. He remembered the thrill of seeing the blood color her bleached-out hair as he pounded her head with the rock. It had been like killing a huge bug.

He walked to Mickey's Bar & Grill a few yards down the road. The music was loud and the lighting was dim. His eyes took a moment to adjust after being in the afternoon sun. He had been free for a solid twenty-four hours. Too much of that time had been wasted. He ordered a rare steak with french fries and a tall cold beer. As he ate, he watched the few people who came and went. To his amazement, a pretty Spanish girl walked into the bar and sat at his table. She wore shorts that barely covered her ass, a tight white T-shirt with no bra, and tall platform sandals.

"You mind if I watch you eat, handsome?" She reached across the table and snagged a fry from his plate.

"If that's what turns you on." Bobby Ray studied the girl openly. She didn't seem to mind. Although her style and manners were on the trashy side, her clothes were clean and good quality. Diamonds glittered from studs in each of her ears as well as a few delicate rings on her fingers. One of them was a wedding ring, but that wasn't his concern.

"I just emptied my old man's bank account, and I'm looking for someone to party with." Her speech was lightly accented. He liked it.

"That depends on what kind of party you're looking for."

"I'm tired of sitting at home while my husband has all the fun. I feel neglected. You wouldn't neglect a woman, would you?"

"No baby, not me, but isn't your old man going to be pissed when he finds his money is gone?"

"I'm sure he will, but I plan to be gone by then." She studied him for a moment. "You look like you're just passing through. How about taking me with you? I don't care where you're going. I just need to grab some clothes from my house, and then I'm ready to run."

"When's your husband going to be home?"

"In about five hours. That's plenty of time to sample what he'll be missing. What do you say?"

Bobby Ray was surprised to find that her house was one of the best in the area. While the girl packed her suitcase, he perused her husband's closet. The guy wasn't too far from his size, just a little wider. A wedding picture on the bedside table showed that he was a heavily muscled black man. Bobby Ray planned to get all he could and be out, before he met the man in person. He filled a large duffle bag with all the clothes and jewelry it would hold. He even found a large box of condoms. They'd come in handy. The girl just laughed when she saw what he was up to.

"What's your name sweetheart?" he asked.

"Juanita, but everybody calls me Nita." She removed a handgun from the bedside table and placed it in her purse.

"I think we're going to be friends, Nita. Take off your clothes."

"I'm always more comfortable without my clothes." Nita pulled her shirt over her head and tossed it on the floor. "What's your name, honey?"

"Bobby Ray."

"I just want you to know, Bobby Ray." She inched her shorts down her legs. "You can't be rough enough for me."

****

Connor worked for two-and-a-half days painting the exterior of the house. He sprayed the siding a robin egg blue color. The white trim was done by hand. He thought about Jordan as he finished the railing.

She'd done a remarkable job of making life seem normal, but she still jumped every time the phone rang or anyone knocked on the door. Mr. Coleman and the Douglases were regular visitors now. Connor had confided in Coleman and Charlie about the danger Jordan and Lizzy were in. He figured he could use all the backup he could get to keep them safe. He was so lost in his thoughts that he almost dropped the paintbrush when the screen door slammed beside him.

"It's about time to get this mess put away and get cleaned up," Jordan announced.

"The sun is still pretty high. I was thinking of putting a fresh coat of paint on those rocking chairs."

"You promised us fireworks, mister, and I intend to see fireworks. Hit the shower."

"Whatever you say, boss." He knew better than to argue. He was happy to see a smile on her face again.

As he carried the blanket and picnic basket to the car, Jordan set the security alarm. Lizzy watched her curiously. "Why do we need the alarm on when we aren't home?"

"We want Tom to be safe while he waits for us to get back."

Jordan and Connor looked at each other without a word before getting in the car. They didn't want to let anything darken their holiday.

****

The park was crowded as they looked for a place to spread out the blanket. Jordan felt as though she were in a scene from an old movie. Everyone in town had turned out to play games and share food.

She noticed that Connor stayed on the blanket under a tree with his hat tilted down. His face was totally hidden by the brim. She had almost forgotten how self-conscious he was about his scars. She filled a plate with the foods she knew were his favorites. As she walked back to the blanket, she saw a woman stop to speak to him. She couldn't believe the feeling of jealousy that came over her. She forced a smile as she approached.

"Hey Connor, I leave for a minute to bring you food and you start picking up women. What's the deal?" Jordan looked at the woman with a forced smile. She was reminded of a modern day Mae West.

"Jordan, I'm glad you're back. I want you to meet Joyce Walker. She owns the beauty salon in town. I don't know how she is with people, but she does a hell of a job on kittens." Connor turned to the woman, "Joyce, this is Jordan Holbrook my, umm, friend."

"Oh! You must have helped Connor with Tom when he found him," Jordan said.

"Your name is Holbrook? Like Patty Holbrook?" Joyce asked.

Jordan was stunned. How long had it been since she had heard that name?

"Well…yes. That was my mother's name. Did you know her?"

"Oh, honey. Your momma and I were partners in crime in high school. I was so sorry to hear she'd passed away. That must have been almost a dozen years ago."

"It will be twenty years in September. Thanks for not saying mean things about her, but I really don't remember her. She left me with my grandparents long before that."

"Well, honey, try not to judge too harshly. Sometimes people get lost in circumstances. Maybe you can come by sometime and let me do your hair. We could talk for a while. Call ahead and I'll cut out some time when we can have a nice private chat." Her smile had softened. Jordan could tell she had a story to tell.

"I think I'd really like that."

Joyce waved and walked away.

"You've never mentioned your mother," Connor remarked.

"I don't know much about her. Maybe it's time I found out more."

The Douglases joined them later that evening to watch the fireworks. Holly begged to take Lizzy home with her for the rest of the weekend. They compromised on letting her go the next morning. Lizzy was already showing signs of exhaustion from her busy day.

Chapter Nine

On Sunday morning, Jordan dropped Lizzy off at the Douglas house. She only stayed for a few minutes before she drove to the cemetery. She wasn't the kind to hang out at cemeteries, but she thought it would be a good place to think for a while.

She hadn't seen Gram's grave since the day of her funeral. The canopy and chairs were gone. The flowers had been taken away. The date of her grandmother's death had been added to the double headstone shared by her and Pop. It had seemed creepy to see Gram's name on the dark polished granite while she was still alive, but now, it was right. The loving couple was now laid to rest, together forever.

Finally, she forced herself to look at the gravestone to the left. Patricia Ann Holbrook, beloved daughter and mother. She'd been thirty-years-old when she'd died. It occurred to Jordan that her own thirtieth birthday was only one month away.

A single dove surrounded by a heart was etched above the inscription. She wondered why she hadn't looked at this grave when she'd been here the month before. She knelt by the headstone and traced the words with her finger. "Who were you, Mom? Why didn't I know you? What happened to you? All I have is questions. I've always been grateful to you, Mom. You knew I would be safe and happy with Gram and Pop.

You knew they'd take care of me. They would have taken care of you, too. Why couldn't you just come home?"

Jordan absentmindedly pulled a few weeds from around the small headstone, and then sat leaning against it. She looked up at the morning sky. "Well, that's all in the past now. I hope Joyce can tell me more about you. I really would like to have good memories of you. I hope you found more happiness in heaven than you did here. Maybe I'll bring Lizzy here someday when she's older. She's a wonderful little girl, Mom." Jordan stood and brushed dry grass and leaves from her legs. "Thanks for everything."

Jordan ran her hand over the cold stone. The next time she came she'd bring flowers to brighten the sad grave.

****

Jordan drove straight into the barn without looking at the house. Connor watched her from under the hood of his van, where he'd been checking the oil. She'd been going into the barn for long periods of time recently. She didn't seem to do anything in there, but he followed her anyway. He wasn't comfortable with her being alone outside the house anymore.

The sun filtered through the holes in the roof. The barn wasn't safe. He needed to repair it before someone got hurt.

He found Jordan sitting at her grandfather's desk in the tack room. Her feet were propped up and her eyes were closed as she lay back in the wooden chair. He lightly tapped on the doorframe.

"What are you doing out here?"

"I was thinking about baking a pie for dessert

tonight. What sounds good to you?" She lowered her legs and sat upright.

"I'm getting to know you pretty well." With hands on hips, Connor tilted his head to study her. "Pies are your comfort food. What's the problem, boss?"

"I'm starting to feel like this barn. Run down, ragged, and empty. I'm just waiting to be torn down, a lot of past but no future. What do I have to offer my daughter besides trouble? Maybe that's why my mother left me here. I don't have anyone like Gram to take care of Lizzy, though. We're on our own."

"You don't need to leave Lizzy with anyone. I'm here to help you. This is going to work out. Look around you. You have a good history here with your grandparents. This is the future they provided for you. It's what you'll pass along to Lizzy. This old place has seen a lot of love. If I have anything to do with it, it's going to see a lot more."

"This old barn sure has seen a lot of love." Jordan smirked.

"You told me the first day I was here that this barn was special to your grandparents."

"My grandfather came out here in the evenings to write his column for the paper. After her chores were done, my grandmother came out to let him know it was time for bed. Most of the time, they didn't wait to get to the bedroom. Sometimes they fell asleep in the hay the whole night."

"How do you know about that?" Connor was astonished she'd have such intimate knowledge.

"My grandmother told me after my grandfather died. She still came out here to think about him at first, but it made her too sad. Finally, she quit coming altogether." Jordan stood to leave.

"She told you that she and your grandfather used to have sex in the barn!"

"They were in love. There isn't anything wrong with loving someone. Thinking about it gives me hope that someday I'll be that happy too."

"It is kind of romantic to think this place was so well used for all those years. I wonder if you'll still be out in this barn making love when you're a grandma."

"I hope so," she murmured wistfully.

"It would be a shame to let an old tradition die, you know." Connor wiggled his brows.

"We're not in love. It wouldn't be the same."

Connor's chest tightened as she walked away. He'd thought his heart had turned to stone, but now it felt like delicate porcelain that had just cracked a little.

On Monday, Connor had finished removing the rotted barn roof. He laid plywood over the exposed rafters. The new roof would go on the next day. As he worked, he thought about the conversation with Jordan the night before. It would be something special to be that much in love. He wished that kind of love for Jordan someday. He longed to be the man to share it with her. However, that just wasn't going to happen. She had made that clear. Could he blame her? Not when he looked in a mirror.

As he sat up to take a drink of water he saw her car coming down the road. His watch showed that it was only three o'clock. Something was wrong. He raced down the ladder to meet her in the driveway.

Jordan glared angrily as she opened the car door for Lizzy. The little girl's clothes were dirty and her hair had pulled loose from the braids on each side of her head. Her bottom lip stuck out indignantly as she kept her head down.

"You're going to stay in your room for the rest of the day, young lady. Be ready to go to bed as soon as supper is finished."

"What happened?" Connor looked Lizzy over for injuries.

"Mrs. Rogers called me and Mrs. Thornton to pick up our kids. They'd gotten into a fight on the playground. Lizzy was still trying to get at the other kid as we were leaving. She's out of control. She gave him a bloody lip and refused to apologize."

"Lizzy honey, why would you do something like that?" Connor asked.

"It's not my fault." She huffed. "Allen is a big bully. He should have to say he's sorry."

"You mean you got into a fight with a boy? And you gave him a bloody lip?" Connor was having a hard time hiding his smile, but Jordan punched his shoulder and frowned. "What did he do?"

"He said mean things about you. I told him I love you and he had better take it back. Then he kept saying, monster lover, monster lover, so I smacked him in the mouth." She folded her arms high over her chest and jutted her bottom lip out again. "I'm not sorry either."

"Your mom is right, Lizzy." Connor's smile was gone now, but his voice stayed calm and even. "She has to punish you. You were a bully today as much as Allen was. Go up to your room."

"I'm sorry, Connor. I didn't have time to ask her how it started."

Jordan looked ready to cry, Lizzy was already crying, and Connor was giving it some consideration.

How had an ordinary day gone to shit so quickly?

"It's not your fault. It's not Lizzy or Allen's fault either. In a way, it's actually my fault. I'll figure out a way to fix things. Don't worry." Connor walked back to the barn and hammered nails until his arm ached. They were all quiet at the table that evening.

Lizzy began crying again on her way up the stairs after supper. "This isn't fair," she complained to Connor. Mom always says to stick up for what's right. She didn't even let me check the mailbox when we got home."

"You're going to have to figure out a way to get your message across without hurting the other person." Connor carried her the rest of the way. It felt good to have someone stick up for him, even if she was just five-years-old. "And don't worry about the mail. I'll check it for you."

Connor opened the roadside mailbox to find a large white envelope rolled up inside. He knew right away that it was trouble. He walked into the kitchen where Jordan stood, running dishwater.

"Jordan, you have a letter from the county courthouse. I think you'd better open it."

"It would be just my luck to be called for jury duty a few weeks after moving here." When she pulled out the notice and unfolded it, her hands started shaking.

Connor read over her shoulder, *Bobby Ray Butler VS Jordan Holbrook Re: Elizabeth Holbrook.* He led Jordan to a chair before he finished reading. He paced the kitchen as he flipped through the pages.

"I'm sorry, Jordan. I should have expected him to try something like this. It just didn't occur to me that he'd think of it, especially this soon. I didn't think he'd take any interest anyway, since you haven't had any contact with him."

"What does it mean?" Jordan looked helpless and confused. "I couldn't even get past his name. What is he trying to do? Can you make heads or tails of it?"

"He's suing you for joint custody of Lizzy."

"Can he do that? He's a convict. He's a violent man."

"I know that, but he's done his time. He's supposedly a reformed man now. He's never done anything to hurt Lizzy or any other child." Connor looked down at the letter to avoid eye contact. "He can try this, but he'll probably only get visitation."

"No. He can't do this. I won't ever let him near her. I'll take her and run if I have to." The desperation was clear in her voice.

"If you do that, you'll only make his chances better. The court would see you as unstable and uncooperative. You'll have to stay and fight. All the court knows, at this time, is that he is her legal father."

"Don't say that. He's never even seen her." Jordan was approaching panic quickly. "I don't even know how he found out her name."

"What does Lizzy know about him?"

"She doesn't know anything. She hasn't ever asked. If she did, I wouldn't know what to tell her. I figured she could live without a father like I did."

"But you had your grandfather." To hell with the rules. Connor pulled her into a hug. "Didn't you ever ask about your dad? Didn't you ever want to know? Don't you still wonder about him? I think I would."

"Yes. I wonder every time I look in the mirror. I guess I was just fooling myself. I've been wrong about everything. Now I know Bobby Ray's out there and I don't know what to do. He's mad. He wants to hurt me in the worse possible way. I can't even think about what he might do to Lizzy." Tears flowed from her eyes as she sobbed against his chest.

Connor grabbed her by the shoulders and forced her to look at him. "You're stronger than this, Jordan. Don't you dare fall apart on me. You just do exactly as I tell you and we'll be okay. This is going to take careful planning. Do you trust me? We only have two weeks. Please, tell me you trust me."

"I guess I do." Jordan sniffed. "I don't know. I haven't trusted anyone in a long time."

"Go upstairs and run a nice warm bubble bath. I'll be back in a few minutes, I promise." Connor watched her walk toward the stairs without a word. She was doing as she was told, no question, no argument. She had subconsciously slipped back into the submissive role her ex-husband had taught her.

After a quick trip to his van, Connor returned with extra clothes and a bottle of whiskey. He set the alarm by the door before he went upstairs with a cup of hot tea. He found Jordan sitting in the tub covered in bubbles.

"Drink this." He handed her the mug. She choked a little, as she tasted the unfamiliar burn of whiskey in the tea. She held the mug in both hands sipping while he ran the sudsy sponge over her shoulders and back. Once finished, he wrapped her in a thick bath sheet and carried her to bed. She was nearly asleep. Mental exhaustion could be as taxing as a day of hard labor.

He pulled a gown over her before tucking her into bed. He couldn't help just looking at her. She was so beautiful. He couldn't stand how helpless she seemed. He wanted the strong, funny, passionate Jordan back. The one he'd known before Bobby Ray Butler was released from prison.

"I'll be downstairs if you need me."

Connor reclined against the headboard in the spare bedroom to think.

He's close; he has to be. I could find him and kill him. He would never expect me to be here. He wouldn't even remember me. I was just one of the many people he victimized.

I could kill him in so many ways. I don't care if I go to prison for the rest of my life. I could get my revenge. Jordan and Lizzy would be safe. Jordan could go on with her life. But, what if I fail? Who would look after them then? Would I then be the same to her as that monster? I would never see Lizzy grow up. Even if Jordan never loves me, at least here I would be near her. I could still watch out for her. No, this isn't about me anymore. I have to help her fight. I have to use the skills I know best.

Chapter Ten

Connor woke the next morning to the sound of an alarm clock in another room. He rolled over to find Jordan lying beside him. He'd stayed awake until the early morning hours, and then fell into a deep sleep, too deep apparently. He couldn't make that mistake again. She had come into the room and slipped into his bed without him knowing. He should have been more alert. If someone snuck up on him now, it could cost him a lot more than a few scars. He'd be risking Jordan and Lizzy.

She was so beautiful. She smelled so good. He wished they could stay like this all day and just forget their problems. He moved against her to bury his face in the sweet fragrance of her hair. He placed a little kiss on her neck. Her whole body shuddered and her eyes blinked open. When she recognized him, she smiled and snuggled closer, letting her eyes fall closed again. The sigh she released made his morning erection twitch to seek its favorite spot.

She rolled over to put her back against his chest. All she wore was a large sleep shirt. He circled her with his arms as he found his way inside her with one smooth push. Her warm dampness was more than he could resist. As he moved slowly in and out, the silky tightness almost drove him wild. One hand messaged her breast as the other found the sensitive bud between her legs. She moved against him in the same rhythm, moaning softly. Her fingers clutched the blanket as her breaths came quicker. Their movements came faster until he couldn't hold back a moment longer. When Jordan ground herself against him, his climax surged through his veins like a freight train.

He lay breathlessly with her folded in his arms for a few long minutes. His heart ached to tell her how much he loved her. He had to get her through this mess, and then he had to leave. It was the only fair thing to do, for them both.

"Jordan, honey," Connor whispered. "I don't suppose you're on the pill are you?"

"Of course not. I haven't had sex since before Lizzy was born."

"Oh yes you have, unless you have another name for it." Connor sat up on the edge of the bed. "We must have done it five times the first time, and here we are again."

"Why didn't you do something? I can't remember everything you know." She sat up on the opposite side of the bed. "It's been a long time since I had to worry about that kind of thing."

"You took me by surprise. I didn't have time to prepare."

"With all the stress we've been under, I'm sure we don't have anything to worry about." Jordan caught her lip between her teeth and paused. "I have to get ready for work."

"By the way," Connor said, before she reached the door. "You're pretty damn amazing for being so out of practice."

"Right back at ya, Romeo." She smiled.

Their hearts were a little lighter, even though Connor insisted on driving her to work.

After he dropped Jordan off, he took Lizzy on to Mrs. Rogers' daycare. The other children stared in silence as he walked her inside. Mrs. Rogers nervously twisted her hands when she saw him approach.

"Good morning. My name is Connor McCrae." He shook her hand. "I heard you could use some help keeping these little ruffians in line this morning. I brought a book I thought they'd like to hear."

"I think that would be a great idea," Mrs. Rogers agreed. "Make yourself at home Mr. McCrae."

By the end of the morning he'd handed out juice, read two stories, and roughhoused with every boy on the playground. At first, the smaller kids had shied away. But they eventually wanted in on the fun too. He promised to come by again the next week, after the kids had all begged him to stay.

Lizzy was the envy of her playgroup—Allen Thornton had been properly shown up—and Connor had made a dozen new pint-sized friends.

"You know, you could handle big people just as easily." Mrs. Rogers laid out mats for the children's' naps. "If you put yourself out for people to get to know, the way you did today, you'd be the most popular guy in town."

Connor simply shrugged and waved goodbye.

After backing out onto the road he pulled out his new cell phone and started the more important work of the day. He knew people in Tampa that would be a big help to him now…if they'd still talk to him.

****

Jordan sat in the break room at lunchtime, stirring a

cup of soup and thinking about her morning. She remembered waking up at about three o'clock, sensing him in the house. Jordan was drawn to him like a moth to a flame. She desperately needed Connor's warmth and strength. She hadn't planned to have sex with him, but once he'd touched her, she needed him more than breath in her lungs. Jordan hadn't ever needed anyone like that before and no one else would do. Only Connor could make her feel this way.

She was getting too attached, too dependent. Connor was a drifter. He'd be moving on, leaving her empty and alone. He'd walk away and never look back. That's the way he lived his life. Jordan was sad to realize that she would never feel this way about another man for as long as she lived.

Bobby Ray was out there somewhere. Connor had made it clear he planned to put himself between them. She felt as responsible for his safety now as she did Lizzy's. Would any of them make it out of this mess in one piece?

****

Bobby Ray stood on the balcony of the small apartment he and Nita had rented with her husband's money. She still had six thousand dollars, but he'd need to find a job if he was going to make a good show for the court. Besides that, it had been part of the agreement he'd made with the parole board. He'd given them a sad story about how desperate he was to see his only baby girl. The parole people allowed him to transfer down here with tears in their eyes...the suckers. He'd do the same with the judge if Jordan didn't do what she was told.

Soon he would have his revenge on the bitch. Once

that was done, he planned to leave the country and never come back. He liked the idea of living in Mexico, if all the little senoritas were as friendly as Nita.

He turned to watch her through the glass door. True to her word, she was more comfortable naked…and she did like it rough. He'd have to lighten up a little on her, if she was going to do him any good with his plans. The bruises and bite marks stood out, even on her dark skin. They wouldn't make a good impression on polite society, but shit, she was game for anything. She even loved his pictures. Not everyone who'd seen them really appreciated his art. That's why he'd hidden them for so long. But Nita actually posed for him sometimes. The only thing she had objected to was his heavy leather belt around her neck. That was okay; he'd save that for Jordan.

He caught a glimpse of his reflection in the glass. Nita had helped him change his image. He looked like a respectable businessman. His jeans and T-shirts had been changed to slacks and light cotton, button down shirts. His dark curly hair had almost touched his shoulders. Now it was clipped to barely more than a shadow. His scruffy beard had been trimmed into a neat goatee. He had a good body. The equipment in the exercise yard had helped him stay in shape.

He couldn't wait to see Jordan's face when he walked into that courtroom.

He wished he could have seen her face when she received that court notice. He'd let her stew over it for a while before he made contact. He was such a good guy; he was willing to give her some options.

Chapter Eleven

Connor pulled away from the bank after dropping Jordan off for work on Friday morning. He'd moved into the house for the duration of the Bobby Ray complication. Every morning he found Jordan curled up in his bed like a scared rabbit. They didn't talk about it, but they both knew how much trouble could be coming their way.

Jordan was changing as time drew closer to the court date. She was quiet and sullen. She couldn't seem to make decisions. She couldn't focus on the simplest task. Just this morning, he had to choose her breakfast cereal. She would have gone to work without her purse if he hadn't thought to grab it on his way out. It was a wonder she could dress herself these days.

He understood that she was under a lot of stress, but she had to pull herself together before the hearing.

Even Lizzy sensed a problem. When she fell into one of her zombie trances, she tried to draw Jordan out. They were almost in a role reversal with Lizzy taking care of her mother. He'd have to talk to Jordan about this soon.

Connor's cell phone vibrated in his pocket. "McCrae here..."

"I've got a list of every visitor and every inside contact the guy had while he was put away. I even have a list of the books he checked out from the prison library." The familiar gravelly voice didn't offer a greeting. His old friend John was all business. "This is a really friendly bunch of people. The guards and employees say our boy was a model inmate, but the other inmates I interviewed don't agree. They gave me a complete rundown on every move the guy made. Now I'm ready to start looking up his old friends and co-workers. Anything else I can do for you, kid?"

"You've done a great job as usual, John. You always were the best. Get all the background you can for me. Send all you have to the same fax number as before. Okay?"

"How do you want me to send the tape and photos?"

"I'll call you back with an address. I want it overnight. Do you still have enough money?"

"Caleb says not to let you worry about that. He has it taken care of. He did ask me to have you call him though. He really wants to hear from you."

"I know. I will." Connor rubbed his left cheek. "I've got to get through this mess right now."

"Okay. I'll talk to you again soon."

"Thanks John, you don't know how much this means to me."

Connor sighed when he pulled into the driveway and looked at the old barn. This had become a bigger job then he'd expected. It was becoming obvious that he needed help to finish, and he had a good idea where to find it.

That evening Jordan sat in front of her untouched dinner staring into space. She hadn't said a word since they sat down. Connor had sent Lizzy to her room to get ready for her bath while he cleared the table. He saw that the mail still laid on the counter unopened. His frustration had about reached its peak.

He threw a spatula into the sink, making a loud crashing sound. He turned when Jordan fell from her chair. She lay on the floor curled into a defensive position with her arms over her head and her eyes closed tightly. He grabbed her arms and pulled her to her feet.

"Look at me dammit. Do I look anything like him? Why are you doing this to us? You shut down just when we need you. Pull yourself together, Jordan. I can't help you if you're like this. If you want to save your daughter, stand up and fight." Connor hadn't meant to raise his voice, but if that's what it took, so be it.

"He's not going to stop until he makes me pay for what I did. You know it's true. Then how am I going to help Lizzy?" she yelled back.

"How are you going to help her by crawling into a hole? I've been busting my ass trying to keep things together. I've taken care of Lizzy, the house, the repair work, the investigation on this asshole, and preparing for the court hearing. I've even had to hire extra workers. What have you done? I told you I'd help you, but I'll be damned if I'll let you melt into a puddle of fear. His days of calling the shots are over. Together we can beat him, but I can't do it alone. You're going to have to face him in that courtroom. Be ready for it."

"I don't think I can."

"Why? Isn't Lizzy worth it?"

"How dare you say that to me? She's my baby. I'd kill or die for her."

"Prove it. This monster is coming straight at her. You're all that stands between them. If you keep hiding, she's lost." His voice was quieter now. She just stared at him. "Lizzy's ready for her bath. Do you want me to take care of it?"

"No, I'm her mother. I'll do it." She turned around to leave the kitchen, and then turned back. "Thanks Connor, for everything."

"No problem, boss." He winked then turned back to the sink full of dishes.

The next morning Connor woke to the sound of the ringing telephone. It was Saturday. He hadn't set his alarm clock. Jordan must have slept in her own bed after their talk.

He picked up the kitchen phone, but Jordan had already answered from the upstairs hallway. He couldn't make himself hang up his extension when he heard the voice of a man on the other end of the line.

"Hey, sugar-boo, did I wake you up?"

"Don't call me that. What do you want?"

Connor had never heard her sound so cold.

"Not even a welcome home for your hubby? You're still a very bad girl, Jordan."

"How did you get this number?" she asked.

"I know everything about you, sugar-boo. I know you inherited money and a house from your granny. I even know you work at a bank." Bobby Ray chuckled in that evil way Connor remembered. He shuddered all over. "I figured you might be a little stressed about the court hearing, so I thought I'd make you a deal instead."

"You want me to give you my money?" Her voice was shaking.

"Let's not forget about the bank, honey." Connor heard the sneer in his voice. He pictured it in his mind.

"I can't take money from the bank." She was panicking again.

"Well, I want you to think about it. I hear that little girl of mine is a real beauty. Does she really look like you? I guess I can find that out for myself when I take her home with me. I've got a room right here in my new place for her. It's got a pretty pink bedspread. She's really going to love her daddy."

Jordan was reaching her breaking point. Connor had to do something. "Hello. Is this Mr. Butler?" he asked.

"Who the hell is this?" Bobby Ray's voice raised several octaves.

"My name is Connor McCrae. I'm Ms. Holbrook's legal counsel. I don't know if you're aware, Mr. Butler, that your proposal is illegal. It's called extortion. The court won't look kindly on this." Connor's voice stayed low and steady.

"You can't prove anything. I'll deny I ever called."

"Well, you certainly could do that, but your call is being recorded on Ms. Holbrook's phone records. Good thing I decided to attach a recording devise to her phone. I wanted you to be aware of that. We should probably save any further conversation for the courtroom. I'm looking forward to meeting you there. I've heard so much about you. Have a nice day, Mr. Butler."

As soon as he hung up the phone, he ran toward the stairs to find Jordan. They almost collided in the middle of the living room.

"Do you think he bought it?" Jordan asked with wide eyes.

"I sure hope so. By the way, you were great." He

grabbed her into a bear hug and spun her around. When her feet touched the floor he was kissing her.

The day had started out badly, but Bobby Ray's voice had done something to Jordan. She tore through the house like a tornado. The beds were changed, laundry was washed and floors were scrubbed within an inch of their lives. The whole time she ranted about the audacity of Bobby Ray's proposal.

"How dare he think I would just hand over everything that my grandparents worked so hard for? Then, to suggest I embezzle money from the bank. He must be out of his mind. And, if he honestly thinks he'll ever lay a finger on my daughter, he'll have a fight on his hands like he's never seen before. I'll kill the son of a bitch."

"Slow down sport, Lizzy is liable to hear you," Connor said in a stage whisper. "I think you rubbed the finish off the floor in that spot."

Carrying her mop bucket to the back door, Jordan tossed the dirty water on a hydrangea bush by the steps. She turned back to Connor not looking as brave as the moment before. "What am I going to do, Connor? I can't afford to make any mistakes. I don't even have a lawyer."

"I made a few arrangements while you were in the twilight zone. Don't worry. We'll be ready. The first thing we'll do is drive Lizzy to stay with the Douglases. If he drops by, he won't find her here. Then I'll take you to your hair appointment. I want you to look perfect when we walk into that courtroom."

"I agree, and I think I'll be ready. I'm working on getting myself back together." Jordan paused. "That thing you call the twilight zone is a relapse of Post

Traumatic Stress Disorder. I was diagnosed after the robbery and trial."

PTSD, he should have recognized the signs. He still had the nightmares caused by the same condition, caused by the same man. Connor closed his eyes and pressed his fist against his forehead, wishing he could punch himself and not look like an idiot.

"I really appreciate you standing by me like this, Connor. I know being in the same room with that psycho will be as tough for you as it will be for me."

"Don't give it another thought." Suddenly Connor was filled with determination. "He'll be on my turf this time. He doesn't have any idea what he's getting into."

Connor's cell phone rang and he pulled it from his pocket.

"You have a cell phone?" Jordan was stunned. "When did you return to civilization?"

Connor rolled his eyes and walked outside before he answered the call. "McCrae here..."

"Hey, boss, it's Ted. I've been having a hard time following this guy and backtracking his movements at the same time, but I think I've got something for you. He left the prison with a hooker named Doris Pritchett. No one has seen her since, but the idiot is driving her car. For all I know, she could be in the trunk. He has another woman with him now. I don't know who she is yet, but I have a good idea where to look. Stay on the lookout for a small, young, Hispanic woman with shoulder length hair and lots of bruises. This guy is a real animal, but she seems to like it. I'm thinking, he may try to send her into places he can't go."

"Yeah, that's good to know." Connor made a mental note to put out the word. "What's he been up to?"

"He's looking for a job. He has an apartment in Venice. I don't know where the money is coming from yet. He's changed his appearance and upgraded his style. I'll send some pictures. As a matter-of-fact, I can fax one over now. Can I use the fax number you gave John?"

Connor thought for a minute. Where did he get all that money? "Do that," he said. "I don't want any surprises. Have you found out who his lawyer is?"

"Yeah, his name is on the list John faxed to you."

"I figured he'd visited him in the prison."

"Nope, he was an inmate there, just got out six months ago. He did time for white-collar stuff. It seems like he should have been disbarred."

"Not necessarily, but I intend to look into it."

"You know," Ted added. "All this back and forth would go a lot easier if you used the internet features on your phone. I could just e-mail the pictures to you."

"I'm sure it would be easier for you, Ted, but not me." Connor was embarrassed. "Do you know how much technology has changed in the last five years? I had to read an owner's manual to figure out how to turn this damn phone on."

"Ha, it sounds like you're the one who was locked away all that time."

"I guess, in a way, I was."

"Well, you're a smart guy. You'll catch on quick. I'm just amazed that you found a fax machine still in use. I hope it belongs to someone you can trust."

"For some odd reason, I believe I can trust this person with my life. And you know that's not something that comes easy for me."

"You know John and I always have your back, boss."

"I'm not your boss, Ted."

"Old habits are hard to break. I sure am glad you're back."

"The jury is still out on that. Don't get too used to me."

"Whatever. I'll talk to you later."

Connor ended the call and walked back into the house. "Do you have a suitcase packed for Lizzy?" he asked Jordan.

"You're not going to tell me about the cell phone? What are you up to? I know I've been in my shell lately, but you seem like a different man. I can't help but feel a little weird around you suddenly." She had a concerned frown on her face.

"I'm only doing what's needed to keep you and Lizzy safe. I don't want to control you or scare you. This will all be over soon. I promise."

"Why would you say that, about controlling me? I never said you'd tried to control me."

When he turned away, she circled around to stand in front of him.

"Because that's what you've been expecting lately. You've reverted to your old life. I've made every decision in this house since you got those papers in the mail. I don't want that role, Jordan."

"Do you really think that is what I've been doing?" Her frown deepened.

"I know it is. I'm glad to help you. But I don't want to own you."

"Exactly what role do you want, Connor?"

"We have a job to do, a big one. It would be a lot

easier if we worked together, like partners."

"Okay then partner, tell me what you're up to."

"Wait until we're alone tonight." He smiled, thinking about being alone with her again. "We'll cook supper together and I'll tell you all about it."

Chapter Twelve

Joyce had a typical beauty salon, cheesy glamour posters on the walls and the smell of permanent wave solution and nail polish. She ran from the back room wearing her usual tight spandex and a high curly hairdo wrapped with a large purple scarf.

"I finally get to play with all that wonderful hair. Sit down and let me do my magic." She put her largest brush to use on Jordan's copper curls. "How do you want it?"

Jordan turned to Connor in cold fear.

"Don't look at me. I don't know about this stuff," he defended.

"Oh, stop the drama." Joyce laughed. "I don't want to change it too much. I mostly just wanted to spend some time with you. I'll take off a few dead inches and give you a super conditioning treatment. It'll do wonders for you. We'll work on your nails and make-up, too. It's on the house. Being Patty's girl makes you the same as family."

"You really knew my mom well?" Jordan asked.

"I sure did, honey. Sit down and I'll tell you all about it."

When Jordan leaned back in the shampoo sink she spotted Connor from the corner of her eye. He picked up a few pages from the fax machine behind the counter and slid them inside a manila folder. She was anxious to find out what he was up to, but the next little while would be spent on another mystery in her life.

"Your momma and I were like two peas in a pod." Joyce sighed. "We were crazy in high school. We went to all the ballgames and double-dated. My folks were just as strict as Patty's, but we always seemed to find a way around them. Not that they were wrong, mind you. We would have both been better off if we'd listened to them better."

"What was my mom like back then?" Jordan asked.

"She was pretty and outgoing. Not an enemy in the world. We were both boy crazy, though. That's every girl's downfall, I guess. That's when we start making bad decisions." Joyce finished washing her hair and moved her to the styling chair.

"Yeah, I guess I can relate to that." Jordan watched Connor sneak out of the salon, big chicken. "Why did my mom leave Mayville? Did you ever hear from her after that?"

"Sure I did. We stayed in touch for a long time."

"Then maybe you know who my father is!"

"Of course I do, honey. Your momma told me everything. I guess it's about time someone told you."

Joyce told her a tale of a young girl and her secret love affair with a soldier. Her despair and loneliness after her soldier was sent overseas and died a short time later. How the girl gave their baby up when she couldn't fill the void his loss left in her heart.

After a good cry, Jordan felt cleansed. She was *somebody* now. She was the daughter of U. S. Army Sgt. Troy Jordan, lost in action just weeks before her birth.

"What's kept you in Mayville all these years?"

Jordan asked to lighten the mood.

"My daddy took off with a younger woman when I was about nineteen and my momma just wasn't the same after that. I still live with her. Then, Arnold Coleman and I started keeping company a few years back. Nothings ever come of it. He only had eyes for your grandma. I don't have much of a life. I live through all the women who sit in this chair, but that can be pretty interesting sometimes."

"You're welcome at my house anytime. Maybe we could get together for lunch once in a while," Jordan offered.

"Oh, that's so sweet of you, but you don't want to hang out with an old broad like me."

"Are you kidding? You're the closest thing to family I have. I promise not to call you Aunt Joyce, but I can't speak for Lizzy."

Joyce grabbed Jordan into a hug then stepped back to turn the chair toward the mirror.

"Oh, Joyce, I love it!"

It was late in the afternoon when they finished and Connor returned to take her home. "Joyce, you must be a miracle worker," he claimed. "I don't know how else you could improve on perfection."

Staring at her on the ride home had almost caused him to run off the road twice. Finally, he pulled his van behind the barn.

Two big, sweaty, mean looking boys were hammering new wood planks to the barn where the broken ones had been removed.

"Who are those boys?" Jordan looked them over suspiciously.

"Oh, they're the Donahue twins, Luke and Leon.

They've been helping me out." Connor grinned. "Believe it or not, they're nice kids. They just need to be kept busy."

"I'll go inside and make them some iced tea and sandwiches. Boys that size always need something to eat."

In the kitchen, she added slices of apple pie to the tray of ham sandwiches and tea. She walked out to the barn to find the boys putting away their tools.

"You can't leave without having something to eat. It looks like you've put in a lot of hard work today."

They both looked at the ground as they shuffled their feet.

"Thank you, ma'am, but momma says we're not to bother you. Mr. McCrae has already paid us for today."

"It's no bother. I'd hate to throw all this out," she coaxed.

"We wouldn't want you to have to do that, ma'am," the other boy mumbled. "I am a little hungry."

"Thank you, ma'am," the first brother added.

Jordan set down the tray and walked back to the house. In the reflection of the window she saw them look at each other with big smiles.

"Now I see why McCrae hangs around here," one of them said."

"Yeah, the food looks good too."

****

Connor inspected their work as the twins ate and set the empty tray of dishes on the back steps. Soon, they retrieved their dirt bikes from the barn and headed home.

Jordan chopped vegetables for a salad as he rolled meatballs at the table beside her. A pot of spaghetti sauce simmered on the back of the stove.

"What did you and Joyce talk about all that time?" he asked.

"We talked about my parents."

"Parents, as in two, a pair? What did you find out?"

Jordan repeated their conversation while she finished the salad and set the table. Connor listened intently from the stove. He expected tears, but instead she wore a satisfied smile.

"It's been a big day for you. I think we should celebrate." He found a bottle of red wine in the pantry and a set of tapered candles in the china cabinet. The sun was setting as he watched her eat. She seemed to be daydreaming. Was she thinking about her parents, her ex-husband? Was she missing Lizzy? "You're awfully quiet tonight. What are you thinking about?"

Her answer surprised him, "I was thinking that I'd like to have more children, maybe two. Do you think this house is big enough for a family that size?"

"Are you thinking about getting married? You know a man can be handy with a thing like that."

"I hope to someday. Do you think I'm too old to have more babies?" She frowned.

"No. You have plenty of time. This house could be bigger. If you tear out the fireplace, you could add a whole section. Another bedroom could go at the end of the hall upstairs. Off the living room, you could have a new den or something. It could be done."

"That fireplace never gets used anyway. Maybe when this trouble is over, I'll give it some serious thought. Which reminds me, you promised to tell me what's going on with you."

Connor took over the conversation while they

finished supper and washed the dishes. Jordan never interrupted. She sat on the sofa looking stunned. She'd learned more about him in the last hour then she had in the weeks he'd been there. She heard about Connor's friends, his family and his life before the attack. Connor McCrae had been an attorney, specializing in family law. Actually, he still was. Lastly, he told her his plan to help her fight Bobby Ray in court. "I guess I should let you have some time to let all this soak in," he finally said. "I'm going to take my shower."

After he returned, she was still sitting in the same place. "Are you bothered by my plan?"

"No. It sounds like you're a lot more prepared for this than I am. I guess it just bothers me that I really don't know you very well."

"So, I wasn't always a handyman. How I make a living doesn't matter that much to you, does it?"

"But, you're a lawyer, a suit and tie, legal briefs, martini lunch, lawyer."

"I'd rather have one of your meatloaf sandwich and iced tea lunches," he laughed. "Don't believe everything you hear about lawyers."

"Connor," Jordan groaned, "you live in a van. No wonder you only charge fifty dollars a week. You're probably loaded!"

"I'm a little loaded," he admitted. "Is that a problem?"

"I don't know if I'm comfortable with you anymore. Your whole family are attorneys. You were probably born in the Taj Mahal."

"Actually, I was born at Tampa General, and my mother is a retired paralegal. We handle divorces, custodies, and prenups. It's not like Perry Mason."

"How much was your allowance when you were twelve?" Jordan asked.

"What?"

"Seriously, I want to know. Did you have to do chores? Did you get grounded?"

"Okay, my brother and I had to do lawn work and wash the cars for ten bucks when we were twelve."

"Cars, not just a family station wagon. You probably had a riding lawn mower too."

"I'm just a man, nothing special." Connor stood and took her hand, pulling her from the sofa. "The only special thing about me is how I feel about you." He kissed her neck and then her shoulder. "Let me show you how I feel."

"I'm not sure how I feel right now."

But Connor didn't get any resistance as he led her to his room and undressed her. They made love until she was exhausted, and then he found his guitar and serenaded her to sleep. Life was perfect at that moment.

****

The next day Jordan decided run a few errands. The court hearing wasn't scheduled until Thursday morning. She needed to occupy her mind with other things. She couldn't stand the thought of being away from Lizzy the whole next week.

After a visit with the Douglases, she and Connor stopped at the store to pick up something for dinner.

"If you'll be all right, I'm going to run to the post office to pick up my mail." Connor wore a concerned expression.

"What can happen to me in the grocery store? There are people all around me."

"Maybe I should stay with you."

"Go away, Connor. It's broad daylight and there must be two-dozen customers inside. I can handle this."

She laughed when he looked back and almost ran into a light pole. After selecting a cart, she headed to the meat section. She intended to make something special that night.

"I thought your bodyguard would never leave," Bobby Ray said as he rounded a corner in front of her.

"Wh-what are you doing here?" Jordan gripped the handle of the cart to keep him from seeing how badly her hands were shaking.

"Haven't you heard?" he sneered. "I've paid my debt to society, thanks to you. I can go wherever I damn well please. You know prison isn't a nice place, sugar-boo. I had a lot of time to think about you. I thought about how you repaid me for all I'd done for you."

"What did you ever do for me? All I remember is a lot of shouting, blood, and bruises."

"Well that just hurts my feelings." He stepped closer to her side. "I found you working in that dusty old office. You hadn't even had a date since you moved to Tampa. I was the only one who saw the potential in you. I gave you a roof over your head and food to eat. I came home to you most nights. But, you had a hard time learning to do what you were told. You had to be punished now and then. I even let you have that baby. You know I could have stopped that if I wanted to. I figured it would settle you down some. Now I finally get out of prison and I find you running around town with another guy. I bet you're fucking him, too. You know you're going to have to be punished for that."

His face was turning red, the way it did when he was angry. "You aren't my husband any more," she whispered.

"Till death do us part, sugar-boo, and I don't plan to die. Things will go my way, if you know what's good for you."

"Is that a threat?"

"I don't need to threaten. If I can't have you, I'll at least have my kid. You could come with her and make sure she stays safe. My new girlfriend would get a kick out of you. We could be one big, happy family."

"If you have a girlfriend, why can't you just go on with your life and leave us alone?"

"You took away too much of my life. You owe me, sugar-boo. You owe me big."

He walked out the door. She gripped the cart handle to keep from collapsing.

****

Connor sorted his small stack of mail as he walked out of the post office. He found a card from his mother. He opened it and read...*All is well here at home. Your dad is helping Caleb out in the office. Retirement isn't all it's cracked up to be. If you ever decide to come back home, I promise I'll get him out of the way, maybe with a trip to Tahiti.*

Caleb tells me you've taken on quite a big project down there. If you need any help, just call. We love and miss you every day. Mom.

Connor always felt homesick when he saw her dainty handwriting. He wished it were that easy to just go home and start over again. She didn't understand how hard it was for him to see Caleb. He hadn't spoken to his brother for more than five years. It had been that long since he'd seen his parents as well.

Connor looked across the street to the grocery

store. An old, light blue Impala peeled out of the parking lot. It was Doris Pritchett's car. The one Bobby Ray Butler was reported to be driving. It was moving fast. It had to be him. He'd been in the store with Jordan. Connor sprinted into the street without even looking. A red sports car barely missed him as he crossed.

Jordan was leaving the store without any bags when he reached the door. Connor was alarmed by how shaken she looked. He yelled at a bag boy behind her to bring a cup of cold water. The boy ran to do as he was told. At the car, Connor guided her into the passenger seat.

"Tell me everything he said, every word," he demanded.

Jordan had a hard time remembering, but she told him enough to make him furious.

"I don't want you to ever worry about this again. I'm not letting you out of my sight. If we don't win in court, I'll get rid of him somehow. I don't care what I have to do."

"Don't say that, Connor. He's not worth it, and neither am I. If he wins, I'll give him what he wants. That's the only way to save Lizzy and everyone else. You didn't see him. He's crazy. I could see it in his eyes."

"It won't come to that Jordan, I promise you. That man will never lay a finger on your or Lizzy as long as I'm alive.

Chapter Thirteen

The next few days raced by. Jordan went to the Douglas house after work every evening to see Lizzy. She pretended to be carpooling with Charlie in case Bobby Ray or the mystery man on the phone was watching. Once Jordan had informed him about the calls, Connor concluded they were connected. It was his guess the strange voice belonged to Butler's attorney.

Holly put a hat over Lizzy's hair and drove her to Mrs. Rogers every morning. Any stranger would think she was just a member of the Douglas family.

With the help of the Donahue twins and Arnold Coleman, the barn had been finished and painted traditional red. Connor and Mr. Coleman decided it would be best if Connor moved his things to Jordan's room. Coleman would move into the guest room until everything was settled. Jordan agreed.

On Wednesday night the three of them had a quiet dinner together, and then Mr. Coleman excused himself to his room. The house wasn't the same without Lizzy's chatter. Jordan was miserable. Connor waited while she showered and prepared for bed. When she came into the room, he asked her to sit with him.

"Do you know what you're wearing tomorrow?"

"Just my blue suit and a white blouse."

"That sounds good. I want you to wear this, too." He pulled a small ring box from his pocket. Inside was an exquisite diamond engagement ring. "It may help your position to appear to have a partner. The court likes children to be placed with complete families."

Jordan slid the ring on her finger to admire it. "Where did you get it? It looks real."

"It is real. I don't want anyone to have any doubt. As far as they're concerned, we plan to marry at the end of the month. Can you go along with that?"

"Yes, I just hope I can hold myself together with everything else. I'm a nervous wreck."

"I know. So am I."

They lay in bed that night staring at the ceiling, waiting for morning. Their futures hinged on every aspect of this court hearing. Every expression, reaction, question, and answer would be analyzed.

The next morning, Jordan spent two hours locked in the upstairs bathroom. She was careful to copy everything Joyce had taught her about how to do her hair and make-up. The make-up took three tries, but the hair was pretty easy. She looked at her reflection in the full-length mirror. Her blue silk suit had a straight skirt that came to the center of her knees. The jacket was waist length with no lapels. Her pumps matched her suit perfectly. The white crepe pullover blouse was a plain, simple style. Her only jewelry was Gram's pearl earrings and Connor's diamond ring.

Connor was waiting at her desk in the living room. He snapped his black leather briefcase shut before he turned to her. "You look perfect."

"Not too shabby yourself." She eyed him up and down as he stood. His hair was pulled back into a neat braid that could be tucked inside his collar. His face was shaved clean to reveal a strong jaw line and expose his scar. He wore a silver gray suit that looked foreign made and expensive. It fit him perfectly. Over his pearl gray shirt was a blue striped tie that made the blue in his eyes stand out. His black Italian shoes probably cost more than her computer. She felt confident just looking at him. "Surely you didn't have that suit in your van."

"Of course not," Connor tugged his cuffs. "I had it sent from home."

"You two look good enough to set on top a wedding cake," Mr. Coleman remarked as he walked in from the kitchen.

"Thanks Mr. C." Jordan gave him a kiss on the cheek. "Wish me luck."

"You don't need luck. You've got right on your side. The judge will see that," he grumbled.

"Well, wish me luck anyway, just in case he doesn't have good eyesight."

"Okay, I wish you luck. Now, you'd better get going. You'll want to get a good parking space."

After a silent drive to the courthouse, they arrived twenty minutes early. They found the appropriate courtroom and sat on a bench outside the door.

"There are a few things I want to tell you." Connor turned to face her. "This is the day the judge decides if the case is worth hearing. Don't get your hopes up that he'll turn it down. Cases involving children are taken very seriously. After today, the judge will hear their side first. That's just the way it's done. It may take a long time, but eventually you'll have your say. Don't interrupt or show too much emotion. They don't like distractions. He'll tell a lot of lies and act totally out of character. He'll try to make the judge think he's the injured party and may say some pretty bad things about you. His lawyer may ask you harassing questions to goad you into losing your cool. Just look at me if you need help. I'll do what I can to get you through this. If it gets tough, just think about the vacation that I'll take you and Lizzy on when it's over. We'll go any place you like, okay?"

Jordan took a moment to gather her thoughts before she spoke. "There's something I want to tell you. I know we don't have any guarantee of how this will turn out. Before it starts, I want to say what I've been thinking, just so you'll know that my judgment hasn't been influenced." She took a deep breath. "I love you, Connor. Even if this all goes wrong, I'll still love you. It doesn't matter if you want to stay working as a handyman or become President of the United States. I'm still going to love you."

Connor stared at her until Jordan began to think she'd made a mistake by confessing her feelings. Suddenly he took her shoulders and drew her close. "I've loved you since the first moment we met, Jordan. You and Lizzy are my heart, the most precious parts of my life." They had time for one quick kiss before the sound of footsteps stopped before them.

Two men stood watching with wide grins. Both wore dark suits and short clipped haircuts. Connor stood to shake each of their hands, looking embarrassed.

"Jordan, I want you to meet my associates and good friends, John Truman and Ted Newsome."

"I'm Ted." The younger, dark haired man shook her hand. "I've been following Butler for the last two weeks. I'm sorry I didn't know you were in that store with him or I would've been there in a flash. However,

I have info on the girlfriend and the money." He handed Connor a folder before turning back to Jordan. "You see, we do the leg work while Connor sits around looking pretty."

"Those days are long gone," Connor scoffed.

"Not from what I saw coming down the hall," Ted replied. "You had this beautiful woman stuck to your face."

"Yeah, I think he's pretty wonderful," Jordan blushed.

"You've obviously never sat across a poker table from him after an all night game, especially if he's losing." The gray haired man held out his hand. "I'm John. I've been dredging up Butler's past. He has quite a history. I'm sorry you had to be part of it."

"We'd better be going in there now." Connor looked at his friends with a stern expression. "You two, make notes of anything you hear that I need to cover. Jordan, you do the same. Let's get this show on the road."

Jordan walked into the courtroom with Connor ahead of her, John to the right and Ted on the left. Several observers were present, no one familiar. Connor looked straight ahead until they reached the front of the room. She was seated at a short table beside Connor facing the judge's bench.

"Who are all these people behind us?" Jordan asked.

"Some may be people working on his side, like John and Ted are for us. But, I doubt he has many resources. Then, you have law students who are gathering information for a paper of some kind. There are always courtroom groupies that don't have a life of their own. And, there may be a few minor news reporters, but this isn't a high profile case. Just don't look back there. It may throw you off."

Movement beyond him caught Jordan's eye. It was Bobby Ray and his lawyer, taking their seats at the table across the room.

Bobby Ray was wearing an ill-fitting dark blue suit. His smile looked evil. How had she ever been attracted to him? There was no doubt that he was handsome. He could still fool a naïve, young girl like she'd been seven years ago. As she watched, she could still feel the long faded bruises and the knife he'd held to her throat. He winked at her. It made her skin crawl.

Bobby Ray's lawyer looked more out of place than he did. He was a short, skinny man with thinning hair and large glasses. His suit fit like a little boy who had inherited his big brother's clothes. His face reminded her of a weasel. Suddenly she realized that she had seen him before. He'd been at the diner, the grocery store, even the gas station. The only difference in him now was the way he was dressed. He'd been spying on her. Anger washed over her. Connor was right. He'd been the stranger on the phone. Remembering Connor's warning Jordan turned to look straight ahead.

The bailiff called them all to stand as he introduced Judge Roy Bender.

The judge was a tall, elderly, black man with a daunting frown. The observers whispered and mumbled as he sat. The judge banged a gavel. "I don't have time for nonsense. If anyone causes a disturbance, they'll be removed from my courtroom," his low voice boomed. He glared back and forth between the two tables. "I've read the reports by both the attorneys in this case. I didn't recognize either of your names, and so I looked into your backgrounds. It seems that you've both been out of circulation for a while." He leaned forward toward Bobby Ray's table.

"Mr. Bennett, I understand that you've been incarcerated for two years."

"That's correct, your Honor," the weasel replied. "However, I assure you that my credentials are still in order."

"Yes, I understand that. I have to tell you, though; I'm not impressed by your list of former clients. I wonder if Mr. Butler is aware of your track record in the courtroom. I wonder if he's best served by your counsel."

"I assure you, sir, that I have given this case my undivided attention. You may even call it a labor of love for a good friend. My only priority is to see that Mr. Butler is united with his daughter."

"We aren't ready to hear the case yet, Mr. Bennett. You and Mr. McCrae are my focus right now. Please sit down." He then turned to Connor.

"Mr. McCrae, I understand that you haven't been in a courtroom for six years. Although your background is definitely impressive, that concerns me."

"Your Honor, I understand your concern." Connor straightened confidently. "I was injured six years ago and hospitalized for a considerable length of time. Since then, I've been on hiatus, for therapeutic reasons."

"I'm just not sure you're ready to give Ms. Holbrook the best counsel after being away for such a long period of time." The judge looked apologetic. "Another attorney has petitioned the court to assist on

Ms. Holbrook's behalf. I very strongly suggest that you accept his assistance."

Connor looked at Jordan with a confused expression. She shrugged with equal bewilderment.

"Your Honor, I mean no disrespect, but we haven't been approached by anyone. There's a lot of material to cover in order to get a co-counsel up to speed."

"You have until Monday morning at nine o'clock to bring him up to speed, Mr. McCrae. I'm recessing this hearing until that time."

A man moved forward from the observers to stand beside Connor. Jordan looked at the briefcase he set on the table. It was a perfect match to Connor's, right down to the little brass plate engraved CM. The man was almost a perfect match to Connor as well. The only difference, his suit was a camel color, his hair was short, and his face was flawless. They stood face to face with identical scowls. Connor was the first to break eye contact lowering his head. His brother's eyes softened and looked away next.

As soon as Judge Bender had left the courtroom, Connor grabbed Jordan's hand and pulled her down the aisle. He didn't say a word as they rapidly walked out of the building to her car. They were half way home before Jordan had the nerve to speak. "Is there something you'd like to tell me?"

"No," he snapped.

She looked back to see the other man following closely behind. They parked in front of the house as Mr. Coleman stepped outside.

"Why are you back so soon?" he asked.

"Ask him." Connor pointed to the dark gray BMW 6 series convertible that pulled in behind them.

The other man got out of the car and stood looking at all of them.

"Holy hell!" Coleman exclaimed. "You've been cloned."

"Why are you driving my car?" Connor angrily inquired of his brother.

"Pardon the hell out of me. I thought you'd like to have it back."

"I don't want it, and I don't want you." Connor stomped up the front steps and into the house.

"You must be Jordan Holbrook. It's nice to meet you." The stranger held his hand out. "I'm sorry I caused so much trouble, but this case seems important to my brother and I'm sure it's important to you. I know he can use my help, but he's too damn stubborn to admit it. I've gone over the information our men collected. I just need to convince Connor to let me in. By the way, my name is Caleb McCrae, you can call me Cal."

"Hi Cal, I'm sorry, I'm still a little stunned. Connor didn't tell me he had a twin."

John and Ted got out of the car that pulled in next.

"Looks like the reunion is over," Ted said. "I guess that means it's time to get to work." They walked into the house. Cal followed.

Mr. Coleman watched the three men walk inside the house and then turned to Jordan. "I guess I'd better figure out what I'm going to feed all these guys for lunch. I hadn't planned on a party."

By the time Jordan reached the living room, Cal and Connor were standing in the middle of the room, toe-to-toe, jackets off, and sleeves rolled up.

"I see you still haven't cut your hair," Cal was

saying.

"Do you still expect me to look just like you? Take a better look, dickhead. We aren't twins any more."

"Try telling that to our mother, asshole. I just think you could look a little more professional."

"Who are you to tell me how to wear my hair?"

"If you two don't sit down, I'll knock you down." John stood and shouted. "I still answer to your father and he would not like this at all. We've got work to do."

"He's right, guys," Ted interjected. "We need to focus on the real issue here, how to keep Lizzy away from that lunatic."

They sobered instantly and sat on opposite sides of the room.

The four men pored over papers and pictures for several hours. Jordan gave up trying to understand all the legal jargon. She knew Connor would explain anything she needed to know later. Finally, John and Ted came to the kitchen to say good-bye.

"We're going to get some dinner and a hotel room in town," John explained. "We'll take turns watching Butler, but one of us will probably be around all weekend. I hope this doesn't put you out too much."

"Are you kidding?" Jordan laughed. "You guys are trying to save my little girl. I can't do enough to repay you for this. Which reminds me, how much am I paying you?"

"You're not," Ted answered. "The firm pays us, *McCrae and Sons Family Law*. You were lucky the day Connor McCrae knocked on your door. They're the best attorneys in the state."

****

Connor and Cal had gone up to Lizzy's room.

"I don't believe I've ever slept in a canopy bed before." Cal shook his head after checking out the miniature furniture. "I think I'll sleep on the couch and keep my clothes in the hall closet."

"You'll probably want to be down there anyway. Jordan is a real bathroom hog. She was locked in there for two hours this morning."

"I've got something I have to ask you, Connor." Cal hesitated for a moment. "You seem to be doing so well now, almost back to your old self. You're obviously crazy about Jordan. I see the look in your eyes when you watch her. You've moved heaven and earth for this little girl of hers. And now, you're back in the courtroom. So why are you still giving me such a hard time? We used to be close. Why do you hate me so much?"

Connor sat on the edge of the bed beside him and combed his hands through the length of his hair before answering. "It's real hard for me, Cal. I'm never going to be normal again. You remind me of that every time I look at your face. The face I used to have. I'm a handyman who lives out of an old van, but Jordan and Lizzy accepted me that way. This morning Jordan told me that she loves me. She's an angel to me. I can't live without her. I want to ask her to marry me when this is over. But then you walked in looking so perfect. It really knocked me off my pegs. I'm not sure she'll feel the same way about me now."

"You don't give her much credit, do you? If she doesn't love you after seeing my pretty face, she never did. But, I think you're going to find out that she does. She doesn't seem like the kind of woman to say things she doesn't mean. She's not Tiffany, Connor. She's not going to kick you while you're down like that superficial little bitch. You've got a real woman this time, brother, and I'm happy for you."

"I really am glad you're here, Cal."

"I know you are, but I've really got to get out of this room. I'm starting to get the urge to play with Barbie dolls."

Chapter Fourteen

On Sunday night, Jordan felt as nervous as she had before the first court date. It had been nice to have all the men to keep her mind busy over the last few days. She'd just returned from spending the evening with Lizzy and the Douglases. It was getting harder every day to leave her behind.

She was standing in the barn door watching the sunset when Connor approached from the house. He looked more like himself in jeans and a T-shirt. At least he looked more like the Connor she knew. She wondered how much he missed his old life. He'd been a little distant since his brother's arrival.

He and Cal had stayed up late every night in strategy meetings. By the time he came to bed, she was sleeping. Maybe she and Lizzy had become too much trouble for him. Maybe he didn't really love her, but just felt a huge sense of obligation. She couldn't blame him if he'd changed his mind about her. Maybe she should let him off the hook.

"What are you doing out here?" he asked.

"I was just thinking." She walked further inside the barn. Connor followed. She slid the ring off of her finger. "I want to give this back to you. I can't lie about something like this. I'm not good at it. Someday, if you want me to have it for the right reasons, you'll give it back to me."

"Jordan, I bought this ring for you weeks ago. I love you so much it hurts. If you walk away from me now, I swear to God, I'll just stop breathing. I can't live without you." His voice broke. "Please marry me, Jordan. I'm begging."

Jordan was stunned to see tears in his eyes. All his confidence seemed to have suddenly drained.

"I'm sorry I hurt you, Connor. I thought you'd changed your mind. I was trying to make it easier for you. I do love you, but I didn't want you to feel trapped."

He looked at her with anger in his damp eyes. "Well, it hurt like hell, so don't ever do that again. Are you going to marry me or not?"

"I'll marry you on one condition." Jordan gave a wicked smile.

"What?" he asked suspiciously.

"I think it would be nice to restart an old tradition." She pulled him into the nearest stall.

"I suppose you plan to have your way with me anytime you like."

"Is that a complaint, Mr. McCrae?" Jordan unsnapped his jeans and lowered the zipper.

"Actually, it was a wish." When she slipped her hand inside his shorts, he groaned. "That's what I'm talking about."

An hour later they walked into the kitchen. Coleman, Cal, Ted, and John were sitting at the table sharing an apple pie.

"We have an announcement to make." Connor grinned.

"I'll be damned!" Cal jumped up to swing Jordan around in a big hug. After returning her feet to the floor he picked a piece of straw from her hair. "There are some things twins can just feel about each other. You'll be good for that old dog."

"I can't wait for the old man to hear about this," Ted whispered to John.

"I know." John chuckled. "He doesn't like anybody to make a decision without his approval first."

****

On Monday morning, Bobby Ray paced the hallway outside the courtroom. "I have a bad feeling about this whole thing. Are you sure you know what you're doing, Bennett?"

"Don't worry, man. The court loves to reunite families. You'll have the kid in your house by the end of the week. There isn't any reason for them to deny your request. You haven't had any history of child abuse or anything. Just be cool and I'll take care of everything." Bennett shrugged casually.

"Don't tell me to be cool. You're the one who had better be cool. If this doesn't turn out right, I'll ruin you. You know what I'm talking about."

"No need to get nasty. I know what I'm doing." After another minute of watching Bobby Ray pace, he asked, "What do you plan to do with the kid? Take her and run?"

"Hell no," Bobby Ray sneered. "I don't want that brat around. I just want her as bait. I'll have that bitch crawling on her knees back to me. Then, I'll make her pay in every disgusting way imaginable."

"That, I'd like to see." Bennett laughed.

"First we have to get past those two lawyers standing guard over her. They look like a couple of serious contenders," Bobby Ray said.

"They have a huge reputation in Tampa. It's mostly the big money, playboy thing though. It doesn't mean a damn thing to a judge down here."

"They come from Tampa? No wonder I keep thinking they look a little familiar. Jordan must have started fucking that ugly one before she moved. Why else would they be all the way down here? She's really moved up in the world. It'll just make it that much sweeter when I knock her back down." Bobby Ray smirked.

****

Judge Bender was announced and seated. He called the room to order.

Bobby Ray strutted to the witness chair wearing the same dark blue suit as he had the previous Thursday. His six-foot-two frame seemed bulkier than six years earlier. The set of his jaw was a little harder. There was a touch of gray in his hair, but the same cold, gray eyes bore into her from across the room. The heat of evil emanated from him. She looked down at the table to break his spell.

Connor pushed a note her way. *Don't look down. Look over his head. He feeds on your fear.*

After Bobby Ray was sworn in and seated he gave his full name and address.

"How long have you been at that address?" Bennett asked.

"Two weeks," Bobby Ray answered.

"Where did you reside before the past two weeks?"

"I was an inmate at the Florida State Prison for five and a half years."

The observers stirred as Bennett let the answer soak into their heads.

"What were the charges against you?"

"Armed robbery and assault."

"Isn't it true that you held you're wife at knifepoint while you robbed a convenience store?"

Murmurs were heard all over the room. The judge banged his gavel once and the room fell quiet again.

"Why would you do such a thing, Mr. Butler?"

"We had a baby coming in a few weeks and we needed the money. I didn't want to take the chance of hurting anyone, but my wife said she would make sure she was careful if I used her as a hostage. I was laid-off from my job and I didn't know how I'd be able to pay the hospital bills. I was desperate and Jordan was insistent."

"You loved your wife, didn't you, Mr. Butler?" Bennett wore a smarmy smile.

"Yes, I would have done anything for her. I still think about her every day."

"You agreed to a divorce only two months after you were incarcerated. Why is that?"

"It's what she wanted. My lawyer at the time advised me that it would be best. I thought I was looking at a fifteen-year stretch. I knew she just wanted to be free to move on with her life. Like I said, I'd do anything for her. I've regretted that decision ever since. If she had ever come to see me, maybe I could have talked her out of it."

"So, she never visited you in prison? Does that mean that you've never seen your daughter?"

"Not one time, sir. I've only dreamed about what she looks like and how it would feel to hold her. She's the only child I have."

"Do you honestly feel you could give her a good

home, Mr. Butler?"

"Yes, I do. I already have a room made up for her in my new apartment. My fiancée has helped me decorate it for her. We plan to get married in two weeks. I hope my daughter will be there."

"How do you plan to support your family, Mr. Butler?"

"I'll be starting a job in road construction right here in town. It's not the kind of work I'm used to, but it's hard to find good jobs after prison. It makes enough money to pay the bills."

"Thank you, Mr. Butler. I have no more questions."

The judge looked to the defendant's table. "Do you have any questions for the plaintiff, Mr. McCrae?" he asked.

The brothers rose and looked at each other, and then Caleb sat down to allow Connor to answer. "No thank you, your Honor. We'll call him back to the stand later."

"Would you like to call anyone else to the stand, Mr. Bennett?"

"Yes, your Honor. I'd like to call Ms. Jordan Holbrook."

Jordan looked at Connor nervously. He gave her hand a squeeze before she stood. Her knees shook as she walked to the witness chair. She sat down and looked across the room. All eyes watched expectantly. She wondered if the pink chiffon blouse and black skirt had been a good choice. She looked back at Connor with doubt written all over her face. He smiled and winked. She wished she had as much confidence in herself as he seemed to have in her.

She was sworn in, and then gave her name and address with a shaky voice.

"No need to be nervous, Ms. Holbrook. We're all just here to decide what's best for your daughter. You want the best for her too, don't you ma'am?"

"Of course I do."

"Can you tell us where your daughter is now, Ms. Holbrook?"

"She's staying with a friend."

"How long has she been staying with this friend?" Bennett asked.

"For nine days." Jordan nearly whispered her answer.

"Did you need a break from your daughter, Ms. Holbrook?"

"No. I just wanted her to be safe."

"You didn't feel that she was safe at your home, interesting. How many people are staying at your house right now?"

She looked at Connor. He patted his hand over his heart. He wanted her to know that he loved her.

"Both Mr. McCrea's and Mr. Arnold Coleman," she replied.

"And your daughter wouldn't be safe with you and these three men in the house. That's quite a crowd." Before she could respond, he continued. "Why didn't you ever visit your husband in prison, Ms. Holbrook?"

"I was afraid of him," she said.

"Let me understand this correctly." Bennett paused for dramatic effect. "You were frightened of him when he was behind bars. But while he was still living at home, you were not afraid to pick up a phone and turn him in for robbing a store, a robbery that you were involved in."

"I wasn't involved," Jordan insisted.

"Did you walk into that store with him willingly?"

"Yes, but I didn't know what he planned to do."

"After the robbery had been committed, you left with him."

She looked at Connor again. He looked down at the papers in front of him, but his hand rose slightly from the table. His second and third finger were curled under to make the sign for, I love you.

"Yes, I did."

"What have you told your daughter about her father?"

"Nothing," she admitted.

"Why not?"

"I didn't want her to be ashamed of where she'd come from."

"Did you think she might be ashamed of what you'd done to him, Ms. Holbrook?"

"No. It was the bravest thing I've ever done."

"You didn't grow up with your parents, did you, Ms. Holbrook? You'd been abandoned, left to be raised by elderly grandparents. You don't know much about how families work."

"That's not true—"

Bennett cut her off before she could finish.

"Your mother left you when you were seven and died of a drug overdose when you were twelve. You hadn't ever been told who your father was. I guess you were lucky to have grandparents to rely on. Your daughter doesn't have grandparents, does she?"

"No," she said in a dull voice.

"I think that's enough, your Honor."

The judge looked uncomfortable. "Do you have any questions, Mr. McCrae?"

Connor stood. "Yes I do, your Honor." He approached Jordan and smiled. "Ms. Holbrook, please tell us who your father was."

She sat up straighter. "My father was Sgt. Troy Jordan, of the United States Army."

"Why hadn't you ever met your father?"

"He was killed in action before I was born."

"Why did your mother leave you in the care of your grandparents, Ms. Holbrook?"

"She was struggling with the pain of my father's death. She didn't want me to be affected by it."

"And how did she die?"

"People who knew her believe that she committed suicide, because of her grief for my father."

"It sounds like they must have been very much in love."

"Yes, they were."

"Your grandmother died recently. How old was she?"

"She was sixty-nine-years-old."

"And you'll soon be thirty-years-old?"

"Yes."

"That makes her forty-six at the time you started living with her. That doesn't seem elderly to me. I've heard of women having babies of their own at that age. Perhaps I'm wrong. What do you think, your Honor? Is forty-six considered elderly?"

Judge Bender gave a rare smile and shook his head. Connor went on. "I've listened to all the questions and answers given today with all my attention. I've made an interesting observation. Not once has your daughter been referred to by name. What is her name, Ms. Holbrook?"

Jordan's whole face broke into a wide smile. "Her name is Elizabeth Holbrook."

"That's a big name for a little girl. She's five years old?"

"That's right. She was named after my grandmother. We call her Lizzy."

"What would you like the court to know about Lizzy, Ms. Holbrook?"

"She's beautiful, smart, and funny. She's looking forward to starting kindergarten this fall, and she has a cat named Tom. She just learned to ride a bicycle. And she has a huge appetite." A few of the female observers laughed.

"Describe the kind of home life you've provided for Lizzy."

"I wouldn't say it's fancy, but we get by. I've worked hard to give her a safe, clean home. She has ample food, clothes, and toys. Even though I've always worked, we spend a lot of time together." Jordan turned to face the judge. "We've only had each other until moving back to Mayville. Now, we both have plenty of friends."

"Ms. Holbrook, can you please explain to the court why Lizzy is currently staying with friends."

"In the last few weeks, we've had problems." Jordan folded her hands tightly in her lap. "It started with anonymous phone calls from someone claiming to be watching us. After I received a summons for this hearing, Bobby Ray Butler called. He suggested I give him money to avoid this case. He even implied that I take money from the bank where I work. More recently,

I encountered him in the grocery store. He said he'd get Lizzy, and if I wanted to keep her safe, I'd have to also stay with him too. I felt threatened when he told me he plans to punish me." Jordan turned to the judge again. "I don't want Lizzy to be hurt because of any of this."

Bennett stood, but before he could speak Connor said, "I think I've heard enough, your Honor."

"Do you have anyone else to call, Mr. Bennett?" the judge asked.

"No, your Honor," Bennett grumbled.

"I have calls to return in my chambers. We'll take a one-hour break before Mr. McCrae continues. I'll expect everyone who wants to be admitted back into this courtroom to be on time." Judge Bender tapped his gavel.

Chapter Fifteen

"What just happened in there?" Bobby Ray cornered Bennett in the restroom as he came out of a stall. "He just made Jordan look like *Rebecca of Sunnybrook Farm*. Everybody in the room loved her when he was finished."

"All that matters is what the judge thinks. He could see that dog and pony show for what it was."

"You tore her down and he built her right back up. That's what I saw. Are you sure you know what you're doing?"

"Yeah, okay, the guy was pretty good, but so were you. I think he just shot his wad. He doesn't have any more to go with. Your testimony was touching. They aren't going to forget that. You'll at least get visitation."

"If I don't, your wife will hear from me. When I tell her all I know, she'll be history, along with her daddy's money. Just remember that."

****

In the courthouse cafeteria, Connor looked up to see Jordan watching him with a serious expression. He gave her a big smile and a wink. She brightened and smiled back.

"This has been hard on Jordan," he told Caleb. "I wish she didn't have to be here for the rest of it."

"You know how these judges can be. He'd call this

thing over if she didn't show. Then, we wouldn't have a snowball's chance in hell of getting rid of Butler."

"We aren't going to get rid of him anyway. Not until he's put away or dead."

"That's why we're still on this investigation, Con. John and Ted are looking as hard as they can to find some way to trip him up."

"I can't keep those guys here indefinitely. They have families to get back to." Connor cocked his head curiously. "You know, I haven't even asked if you have a family yet, Cal."

"Close, but no cigar. That's a story for another time, though." He didn't look up as he snapped his laptop closed. "We'd better get back inside."

Connor walked over to Jordan and put his arms around her. He whispered in her ear as they walked back to the courtroom, "It's going to get really nasty in there now. You know I'm going to do anything I have to, to tear him apart. Can you handle it?"

"I can handle anything that will save Lizzy, especially if you're there."

"I don't know if you understand how bad this may get. Let me say now that I'm sorry if any of this hurts you. I'd give anything for you to be spared from all of this."

"I love you, Connor. It's going to be all right."

"You're an amazing woman, Jordan. I'm so lucky to have you." He kissed her hard on the lips. "Let's get this over with."

Ted leaned over the railing to hand Connor another folder as they sat down.

"You understand that you're still under oath, Mr. Butler?" Judge Bender asked as the proceedings resumed.

"Yes I do, your Honor."

"You may proceed, Mr. McCrae." He nodded to Connor.

"Mr. Butler, I would like to go over some of your previous testimony. You stated earlier that you had been laid off from your job before the robbery occurred. Where had you been working?"

"West Coast Construction Company in Tampa," Bobby Ray answered.

"You and Ms. Holbrook were both employed there. Am I right?"

"That's correct."

"I have pay statements here, for the entire time that you were employed there." Connor held them up at shoulder level. "I have Ms. Holbrook's pay statements as well. They show that you clocked in and out every day until the day you were arrested. The two of you together were making a considerable amount of money."

"There must be some mistake with the dates on those papers. Our expenses were high. We were dead broke."

"What are the chances that your bank would make the same mistake in the dates? Let's have a look at your bank statements for that year." Connor removed the mentioned statements from the folder. "They show your balance at the time of your arrest. It looks like you had a nice little nest egg put away. You must have a good head for finances, Mr. Butler."

"No, there must be some mistake," Bobby Ray insisted. "I don't know where you got those papers."

"They were obtained from the bank by the joint

account holder, Ms. Holbrook. I'm sure they're in order. I'll hand them over to the court to look at. We'll see what they think." He handed the stack of papers to the bailiff. "You have your finances in order now though, isn't that what you said? You have a job to help support Lizzy?"

"That's what I said," Bobby Ray groused.

"What is the name of your new employer and how much money have they offered you?"

"I'll start next week with Reynolds Construction."

"So you haven't had any income so far. How much money have they offered to pay you?"

"We haven't discussed money yet, but I know it won't be as much as I made in Tampa. Things are tougher, now that I'm an ex-convict."

"We don't have any way of getting documentation from Reynolds then, do we?"

"No," Bobby Ray sneered.

"Do you see the man sitting directly behind my brother, Mr. Butler?"

"Yes."

"That man is Mr. Adkins. He's the human resource manager for Reynolds Construction, the only road construction company in town. He brought your application with him today. He says he has an appointment to interview you next week. You haven't been offered a job yet."

"I have a lot of experience. I know they'll hire me."

"Even though you've been convicted of a felony?" Connor asked. "You did include that on the application, didn't you?"

"I don't remember. I may have missed that."

"It's an honest mistake," Connor smiled. "Sometimes those little boxes are hard to find. But now I'm wondering how you paid for a new apartment? The deposit, utilities and furnishings can be expensive."

"My fiancée has been helping me out."

"Oh yes, you mentioned before you're getting married in two weeks. Congratulations. What is the lucky girl's name?"

"Juanita Granger."

"I know a man who lives nearby named Henry Granger. As a matter-of-fact, he's here today to follow up on a police report. It seems someone stole his clothes, jewelry, and even cleaned out his bank account a couple of weeks ago. He thinks it was his wife. She disappeared the same day. You know, I think her name was Juanita, too. But it couldn't be the same woman, could it? She wouldn't be free to marry anyone when she's still married to Mr. Granger. But, that's beside the point now. The police got a tip on where she's staying and they picked her up this morning. Still, it's quite a coincidence. I'll have to introduce him to you when we leave."

Bobby Ray turned as white as the shirt he wore...the shirt that belonged to the man outside the courtroom. Bennett jumped to his feet. "I object, your Honor!"

Before the judge had a chance to reply, Connor turned to Bennett. "You're absolutely right, I've gotten off track. Sorry, your Honor." Connor walked back to the table to set the folder down. "Now, I'd like to know more about the convenience store robbery. I happen to have a copy of the video surveillance tape."

"I object, your Honor." Bennett was once again on

his feet. "None of this has anything to do with the child in question."

"I'm only going over the testimony that Mr. Bennett has already introduced, your Honor." Connor shrugged.

"That's true Mr. Bennett. You're overruled."

The room was abuzz when two deputies wheeled in a big screen TV. Connor made eye contact with Jordan as they hooked up a VCR. She nodded to him with a sullen expression. Cal put his arm around her. As the tape began, she buried her face in his shoulder. The section of tape was over in less than two minutes.

"I have a few questions about that video," Connor stated. "It appeared that Ms. Holbrook was screaming and struggling during the robbery."

"It was all a part of the plan," Bobby Ray replied.

"You pushed her in front of you on your way out of the store."

"She couldn't keep up on her own."

"The video wasn't very clear to me, so I had a few still shots made from it." Connor retrieved eight-by-ten photos from his briefcase. He held one up. "Here's one of you leaving the store. It appears that you still had the knife pointed at Ms. Holbrook, but now it's down at waist level. Didn't you say that she was only a few weeks from having a baby?"

"Yes. I guess I was careless with her. It must have been all the adrenalin."

"Now here's a close-up of Ms. Holbrook in front of the cash register during the robbery. She sure looks frightened to me. There are tears on her cheeks. By the way, what had happened to her eye and mouth?"

"She'd walked into a door frame a few days

before," Bobby Ray answered.

"She must have walked into it a couple of times to hit her left eye and the right side of her mouth. Isn't it funny how the bruising is round and scattered. You would expect a doorframe to leave straight marks. These look like knuckle marks to me. Was she always so clumsy?"

"She had a lot of accidents, yes."

"The nearest emergency room to your apartment was St. Joseph's. We have a copy of her records from there." Again, Connor reached inside his briefcase. "She was in the ER six times. Each time, they listed a variety of injuries. Abrasions, contusions, broken ribs, even a concussion where she'd lost consciousness. And this had all taken place during the time that she was pregnant. It's a wonder that baby survived. You might even think someone didn't want her to, maybe even hoped she wouldn't."

Bobby Ray's face was red and sweating profusely. He had just about reached his limit. Connor wanted to push him over the edge. "I sure hope she's more careful while she's having my baby. Did I forget to mention that we're engaged?" He turned to Jordan. "Show him the ring, honey. She's a beautiful woman, isn't she?"

Bennett leapt to his feet, pounding his fist on the table. "I object!"

Bobby Ray dove over the rail in front of his chair and lunged past Connor and toward Jordan. "I'll kill you, you cheating bitch. I'll kill you and that fucking kid of yours. I should have taken you out before she was ever born."

Caleb held her behind him until the deputies had him handcuffed. Bobby Ray screamed obscenities and threats as they dragged him from the courtroom. The judge banged his gavel to silence the excited observers.

"Mr. Bennett, I believe your client may need your assistance. Mr. McCrae, please approach the bench."

After Bennett had followed Bobby Ray out of the room, Judge Bender and Connor spoke in lowered voices. "Connor, you know you goaded him into that outburst."

"Yes sir, I did, and you enjoyed every minute of it."

"Yeah, it was pretty cool," the judge admitted.

"How long can you hold him?"

"Not very long, I'm afraid. Bennett will claim that he was under undue stress. But, I can get you some restraining orders." He began writing in a notebook. "I guess Butler is lucky in a way."

"How's that, sir?" Connor asked.

"He doesn't have to face Mr. Granger today."

"Can we do anything with that situation?"

"I'm afraid not," the judge replied. "It sounds like the wife initiated the whole thing.

You know I'm going to rule against him, but I have to appear to think it over. You'll get my ruling by the end of the day."

"Thanks, your Honor. I'm going to take Jordan home as soon as you call this thing over."

"You got it."

As they left the courthouse, Connor told Jordan the good news.

"I can't believe it," she exclaimed. "He lost? I don't have to worry about him anymore?"

"I never said that. We're going to have to watch our backs for as long as he's still out there. A restraining order is only a piece of paper. Don't lose sight of that fact. He's pretty damn pissed off."

"So what do we do now?"

"I'd say it's time Lizzy came home. We'll have to watch her like a hawk, but she can't stay at the Douglas's forever. I don't know about you, but I miss that little munchkin."

Chapter Sixteen

Lizzy chattered all the way home about the fun she'd had with Adam and Craig. She'd learned to tie her own shoes and make Kool-Aid. Miss Holly had said that Tom looked like dryer lint and Mr. Charlie gave her a piggyback ride every night on her way to bed. But, she also said she'd missed her room and her swing.

As soon as the car stopped in front of the house, she jumped out and ran inside. She skidded to a stop and backed up a few steps, finding herself faced by three large strangers. Mr. Coleman came from the kitchen wiping his hands on a dishtowel. "I sure am glad to see you, Lizzy. It stinks being the only person in the house under six-feet tall."

Ted slid off the couch to kneel eye-to-eye with her. "Hi Lizzy, my name is Ted." He motioned behind him with a thumb. "This guy, John, and I have been working for your mom and Connor. We sure are glad to meet you."

"How come all you guys are wearing suits like Connor?" she asked meekly. "Did you go to a funeral? When Gram died, all the men wore suits to her funeral."

"No, we had business to take care of. It was a good day. Your mommy must be so happy to have you back home."

Jordan entered with Lizzy's little suitcase. Lizzy hugged her legs still looking at all the big men.

John stood and walked toward the door. "Ted and I are going to get back to the hotel and change clothes. We want to start our surveillance shifts while we still know where Butler is. Where's Connor?"

"He's right behind me. He wanted to park the car in the barn." After the two men walked outside, Jordan looked down at Lizzy. "What would you like to have for dinner tonight, sweetheart? You can have anything you want. I'll go to the store and get it." Lizzy still clung to her legs staring at Caleb. "Did you hear me Lizzy? You can have anything you want for dinner."

"Shrimp, the crusty kind, and french fries with ketchup," Lizzy finally answered.

****

Connor came inside carrying Tom. Lizzy climbed up his body and circled her arms and legs around him. He almost lost his grip on the squirming cat. "What's the problem, monkey girl?"

"There's a man over there that looks like you, but his face is plain," she whispered.

"That's my brother. His name is Cal. Don't you like his plain face?"

"It's okay, I guess," Lizzy shrugged.

"What's wrong with it?"

"Nothing, but I like yours better."

"Why?" he asked, surprised.

"Because, it makes you special." Lizzy cupped each side of his face with her tiny hands. "I love your face."

Connor was so overwhelmed he couldn't speak. He just hugged her tighter and kissed her head. Once the lump in his throat cleared, he said, "I love you too, monkey. I missed you an awful lot around here."

"I'll be clearing out of here today," Mr. Coleman interrupted. "I need to get back to my own place. My garden must be overgrown with weeds by now. Call me if you want me for anything."

"You're welcome to stay for dinner, Coleman," Connor offered. "There's always plenty."

"No, I'm kind of looking forward to some quiet time. Thanks though." He retreated to the spare room to pack his few things.

"If you two don't mind, I'd like to stay on for a little while." Caleb stood. "I haven't had a chance to do anything but concentrate on the case since I got here. I'd kind of like to get to know my new extended family a little better."

"You're welcome to stay for as long as you'd like," Jordan was quick to assure him. "I think you and Connor have some catching up to do, and it looks like the guest room is available again." She walked out the door with Connor close on her heels.

"Where are you going?"

"I told Lizzy she could pick what we'd have for dinner tonight," she answered. "I have to go to the store."

"You're not going alone, are you?"

"Yes, I am. Bobby Ray will still be wrapped up in paperwork at the county jail. This is my chance to go out alone for the first time in forever."

"Well, I guess you're right, but we have a ton of food here. Why do you have to buy more?"

"Lizzy wants shrimp for dinner and we don't have any."

"Didn't Cal say anything?" Connor frowned.

"No. Why?"

"If he eats shrimp you'd better have an ambulance on standby. He's got an allergy to shellfish."

"Oh damn, is there any limit to the way you men will spoil that child? I said she could have anything she wanted for supper. He must not have wanted to disappoint her. What do I do now?"

"That's easy. Just pick up some steaks—surf and turf. That's what Mom does."

"I think I'd like your mom."

"I'm not ready to find that out yet," Connor remarked with a cocked brow.

****

Bobby Ray stepped out of the jailhouse in time to see the old Impala being towed away. "Shit! What am I going to do now?" he asked Bennett. "I can't get the car back. I don't even own it. At least none of my stuff was in it. Luckily, I've got Nita's money in my pocket. I guess I'll have to get a used car from one of those buy-here-pay-here lots down the street."

"Just try to keep a low profile," Bennett advised. "I'm sure you already blew the custody case."

"Jordan is causing me way too much trouble. First jail, and then restraining orders, and now my car. I've even lost Nita. I'll have to get my entertainment and money the hard way. Nita was going to come in handy soon, too. Jordan is going to pay for this. I'm not just going to make her suffer. I'm going to make her wish she'd never been born. And, I want that asshole boyfriend of hers, too. He humiliated me in that courtroom." What Bobby Ray didn't tell Bennett was that he was also in his crosshairs.

After the two men parted, Bobby Ray found a beat-up, late model, economy car at the back of the nearest used car lot. It looked like it had seen its share of wrecks, but it still ran well. He talked the salesman into letting him drive it off the lot for a thousand dollars. He knew the guy was going to pocket the money. The car probably didn't even have a title. But, at least it had wheels.

Back at his apartment, Bobby Ray looked over the mess Nita had left as he sipped a beer. He wondered how much she would implicate him in her legal trouble. He planned to pack up and get the hell out of there. There was just one thing to do first. Bobby Ray looked through his wallet to find a phone number he'd been holding for a while.

"Hello."

"Hello. Is this Mrs. Bennett?"

"Yes, who is this?"

"I'd rather not say, ma'am. All I can tell you is, I'm a concerned friend. I felt you needed to know what your husband has been up to for the last few years."

"What are you talking about?"

"I was in prison with him. I hate to be the one to tell you this, Mrs. Bennett, but he was a prostitute while he was there. He told me that he'd been doing it on the outside for years. I'm told that he would do anything for money or favors."

"I don't believe you."

"Well, I don't have firsthand knowledge, of course, but I am concerned for you. I think you should try to get his medical records from the prison and see a doctor yourself."

The line went dead. Bobby Ray sat back with a smile. Bennett thought he still needed him. He wouldn't suspect that he'd carried out his threat. His wife's daddy, being a big shot surgeon, would have those records by the end of the day. Then, Bennett would be done. Nobody crossed him and got away with it.

****

Jordan finished the dinner dishes and folded the last of the laundry. The sun had gone down and Connor was putting Lizzy to bed. It was nice to have her world back in order for a while.

As she climbed the stairs to give her daughter a goodnight kiss, she heard the music coming from Lizzy's room. It sounded different tonight. She stopped in the doorway.

Connor had Lizzy in his lap sitting on the bed, while Caleb sat cross-legged on the floor, playing guitar. Connor was singing an old John Denver song, *Sunshine on My Shoulders.* She waited as he finished. Then Caleb took over singing *Back Home Again.* Neither man was ashamed to have their deep, rich voices heard. They had certainly been raised in a home where self-expression was encouraged. These men would provide a good environment for her daughter. Jordan secretly wished she could meet their parents. She could learn to be a better parent through them. Connor had made it obvious that he didn't like the idea, when she mentioned it earlier that day. Maybe, now that Caleb had broken the ice, he'd change his mind.

Once Caleb had finished his song, she crossed to the bed and kissed Lizzy good night.

"It's time to end this concert and let this child sleep," she told the brothers. "It's been a long day. You two will have plenty of time to spoil her tomorrow."

Lizzy bounced with excitement. "Can I spend all day with Connor and Uncle Cal?"

142

Jordan looked at Cal with raised brows.

"Hey, she asked and I couldn't say no. It'll be official soon anyway."

"Tomorrow she's going to daycare and I'm going to work. You guys will have to find something to do with yourselves."

"We're planning to build a couple of picnic tables," Connor informed her.

"What do we need with two picnic tables?"

"Cal and I were talking earlier about how much help the Douglases and Coleman have been. You and Joyce have gotten close. John and Ted will be leaving soon. We thought it would be a nice idea to have a cookout this weekend. What do you think?"

"Do you think you could build a barbeque grill too?" she asked sarcastically.

The two brothers looked at each other, and then back at her. "No problem," they said in unison.

The next day was busy at the bank and Jordan came home exhausted. She was surprised to find the house empty. The only sign of life was the smell of dinner in the oven and male laughter in the back yard.

Jordan almost fell out the door when she opened it onto a large bare space. Her steps had been removed along with a huge section of her lawn. Bags of mortar were laid over piles of stone. Connor and Cal were chasing the Donahue twins with a water hose. They were all shirtless, only wearing baggy shorts. Their tanned muscles glistened in the sun.

Mr. Coleman stood off to one side with Lizzy, shaking his head.

"What's going on here?" Jordan asked.

"The boys said you wanted a barbeque grill.

They're putting in a whole damned patio to build it onto."

"What do you think of all these changes, Mr. Coleman?"

"I think the place is looking great, and I think your grandma would be pleased as punch. That's what you're really wondering, isn't it?"

"You know me better than I thought."

Chapter Seventeen

Preparing the new grill for the Saturday afternoon cookout gave Connor a little quiet time to think. It was a special celebration for his engagement to Jordan and winning Lizzy's custody case. Even more than that, it was a blending of old friends and new, old family and new. The only people missing were his parents. They'd get such a kick out of the party. Maybe it was time to take another step back into his past. He knew family was important to Jordan. She and Lizzy only had each other when he'd found them. Also, he had to admit, he missed his mother like crazy. He always had, but being with Caleb magnified the feeling.

His melancholy subsided a bit when their first guests arrived. The Donahue twins rounded the house carrying a cooler between them. Chances were, it was filled with their favorite soft drinks. Caleb approached with a wide grin.

"Doesn't it figure those boys would be the first to show up when free food is on the table?"

"Yeah, do they remind you of anyone?"

They laughed, thinking back to when they were teenagers.

John and Ted were the next to show up.

"Are you sure it's cool for both of us to leave our post today?" Ted asked.

"Butler hasn't made a move for days. He knows

we're looking for him. We're all here with Jordan and Lizzy. He wouldn't dare try anything with this many people around. Besides, we need to get used to not having you guys to protect us," Connor replied.

"We'll be hanging out for a few more days to tie up some loose ends," John informed him. "Then, we'll head home. No telling how much trouble that son of mine has been in. Laura says everything's fine, but it's about time I checked on things firsthand."

"I hope you know how much this has meant to us, guys." Connor was interrupted by activity coming from around the house.

"Who's the woman with Coleman?" Cal asked.

Joyce was in another tight spandex outfit and high heels. Her abundance of curly hair shined brightly in the afternoon sun.

"Good gracious, Connor," she yelled from across the lawn. "You didn't tell me you were part of a matched set. The testosterone level in the atmosphere is positively intoxicating. Somebody get me a beer."

Next Jordan and Lizzy came out of the house. They both wore their hair back in French braids and were dressed in shorts and peasant blouses. Connor looked at Jordan's tanned shoulders and long legs with an approving smile.

"Maybe I'd better lock the barn doors." Caleb shoved his brother's shoulder.

After the grill had been covered with hotdogs and hamburgers, the Douglases arrived. Adam and Craig ran to the patio, followed by their parents. Holly and Charlie were holding hands and grinning like a couple of teenagers.

"I hope we're not late," Holly said.

"Yeah," Adam chimed in. "Mom and dad woke up super late, and then they took forever to get ready."

Both parents blushed and hurried the children away.

Connor outdid himself on the grill and made sure everyone had plenty to eat. Afterward, he lounged in a hammock with Jordan beside him. For a while he watched Adam toss a baseball up in the air, over and over. He was about Adam's age when he'd joined little league, and played baseball until he reached law school. He still loved the game.

"You know, I remember seeing a bat just inside the barn," he told Jordan. "I bet we have enough people to put a couple of small teams together."

Charlie indicated his amputated arm. "I'm no good with a bat, but I'm a hell of a pitcher."

Straws were drawn for teams. On one team, Connor picked Luke, Holly, Adam, and Ted. Cal countered his choices with Jordan, Leon, and John.

"Why do you get five players?" Jordan asked Connor.

"Adam and Holly put together equals one player," he laughed.

"Hey!" Holly objected.

"What about me?" Lizzy asked.

"You and Joyce can be the cheerleaders," Coleman suggested. "Craig and I are the coaches."

They played five innings and the score was five to eight on Cal's side when Charlie called the game due to a sore shoulder. The sun was fading when Jordan brought out ice cream. Everyone settled into a quiet, laid-back mood.

Connor and Caleb brought out their guitars. They

entertained the group with a variety of Country and Southern rock songs until it got too dark to see their strings. It had been the best day Connor could remember. He was disappointed when everyone began to leave.

"Go upstairs and brush your teeth for bed," he told Lizzy. "We big people have a lot of cleaning up to do. We'll come to tuck you in, in a few minutes."

"Okay," Lizzy agreed drowsily.

Connor could tell by her slow stroll that she was ready for a good night's sleep, but a moment later shrill screams came from the second floor of the house. He raced inside the house nearly knocking Caleb down as he passed him.

Connor and Caleb looked over the scene in the bathroom, waiting for the police to arrive. Lizzy's kitten, Tom, lay bloody and lifeless in the sink. The smell of rubbing alcohol made their eyes water. On the mirror the name *McCrae* was written in the cat's blood.

"I guess we should have known we'd be targets now," Cal said.

"I think this one was meant for me." Connor pointed to the cat's face. It had been sliced from the top of his left ear all the way down its stomach.

The police took fingerprints and pictures while a detective asked questions downstairs. They were all aware of what had happened in the courthouse earlier in the week. No one had a doubt who had done this horrible crime.

After three hours, the house was cleared. Connor and Jordan lay sleepless in bed.

"He was in my house," Jordan finally whispered.

"We should have locked the front door while we

were all in the back yard. We won't make that mistake again."

A light tap came on the door.

"Can I come in with you guys?" Lizzy's voice was raw from crying.

"I'm sorry, Connor. I've got to stay with her tonight." Jordan reached for her robe.

"No, wait." Connor rose to the edge of the bed and pulled on his shorts. "We all stay together." He opened the door and carried Lizzy to the bed, laying her between them. "This is just for tonight, okay, monkey?"

"I don't know why people have to die," Lizzy whispered after a moment.

"They just do, Lizzy. Your gram will take care of Tom up in heaven."

"Who killed my Tom?"

"A bad man," Connor told her. "That's why we have to watch you all the time, at least until the police can find the bad man."

"Who is he?"

Connor looked over at Jordan and saw that she was fighting back tears.

"He's a man that your mommy knew a long time ago. He doesn't like her. He wants to hurt her and maybe us too. I know that's scary, but you should know that so you can be extra careful."

"Why doesn't he like Mommy," Lizzy whined. "Everybody else likes Mommy."

"He's crazy, honey, sick in his brain. I don't know why."

"Is he the man who used to be my daddy?"

"Why would you ask that?" Connor brushed the hair from her damp cheek and kissed it.

"I heard Mrs. Rogers talking to Miss Holly. She said my daddy was crazy."

"What else did she say, monkey?"

"She said she was scared when I'm there. Miss Holly got really mad and said that maybe Adam and Craig wouldn't go there any more, if I didn't go there too."

"How would you feel about hanging out here with me and Uncle Cal for a while?"

"That would be lots of fun. I wish you were my daddy instead of the crazy man, Connor. Why can't I call you daddy?"

Connor looked at Jordan again. She looked back as if she were also waiting for an answer. "Would that make you happy, monkey?"

"Happier than anything," she claimed.

"I guess you can do that then."

"Okay." She let out a big yawn and was asleep almost instantly.

****

Bobby Ray peeked around the edge of the drape to see who was knocking at his door. It was Bennett, dammit! He didn't have time for this. The cops could be pulling in any minute. He was careful not to leave fingerprints at Jordan's house, but it wouldn't take a rocket scientist to know he'd been there. Even if they didn't have evidence, they'd at least want to question him. He wasn't in the mood for that bullshit. His camping gear was already in the woods. He'd just had to pack his sketches and was ready to take off. He released the chain at the top of the door and opened it.

"I told you not to come here, asshole."

"I need my money, Butler. You promised to pay

me—what the hell is that smell?" Bennett's lip curled with revulsion. "Is that rubbing alcohol? What did you do, bathe in it? That shit'll dry your skin, you know."

"Look who's giving me advice about cleanliness."

"I don't care if you make your coffee with it, I just want my money."

"I don't owe you a dime." Bobby Ray grabbed his duffle bag and pushed past him out the door.

"I've spent weeks working on your case. Now, I'm broke. Everything I had paid for: gas, food, and lodging. You were supposed to cover my expenses as well as my fee." Bennett jogged down the stairs to the parking lot on Butler's heels.

"You lost the case. I'm not paying you anything."

"You're the one who went apeshit in the courtroom and lost the case."

Bobby Ray tossed the duffle bag into the back seat of his beat-up car and slammed the door.

"I don't even have enough money to get home. What do you expect me to do?"

"Call your wife," Bobby Ray shrugged. "She's your cash cow, isn't she?"

"What am I supposed to tell her? I've been gone for weeks and I don't have anything to show for it."

"Call her, right now, be creative." Bobby Ray reached under his shirt and pulled out Nita's gun. "Put it on speakerphone. I want to hear every word."

Bennett's hands shook so badly he nearly dropped the phone as he opened it and punched in his home number. His voice was remarkably calm when he spoke. "Hi honey, listen, I'm stranded down in Ft. Myers. The car broke down and it cost me a fortune to fix. I need you to wire me some money to get home."

"You're not coming home, Jerry." His wife's voice sounded dull. Butler wore a phony surprised expression.

"Of course I am. I'm finished with my business here and I just need some money to get home. I think my credit cards must have gotten ruined, none of them work anymore."

"What business are you finished with, Jerry?" She didn't seem to have heard his last statement. "The legal business or the prostitution?"

"What are you talking about?"

"You know damned well what I'm talking about. I've got your medical records here from the prison."

"Listen honey, all kinds of things happen to people in prison. You know that."

"The report tells everything, Jerry. You were HIV positive when you got there. You started the medication the year before. When were you going to tell me? Now, I have to be tested. I'm not sending you a dime," she sobbed. "I don't want you to ever come back here. I may be dying because of you. You married me knowing your condition and never said a word. You didn't give me a choice, Jerry."

"Do you think I had a choice, Deb?"

"You made your choice the first time you accepted money for the disgusting things you did."

"Well at least one of us is good at it," he snapped.

Butler didn't say anything, but his shoulders shook with quiet laughter.

"You sound proud to be a prison bitch."

"I've never been anyone's bitch, honey. I was paid too well, even by you. And that was the hardest one to take, you ugly pig."

"I'm bringing charges against you, Jerry. You'd better stick with the prostitution because I'll make sure you never practice law again." The phone went dead.

Bennett stood, frozen in place, still holding the cell phone in his hand. His pale face actually took on a green tone.

"See you around, bitch." Bobby Ray laughed as he tossed his keys in the air and caught them.

Chapter Eighteen

Jordan kept picturing Bobby Ray, walking through her front door and up the stairs. What if Lizzy had been in that bathroom when he opened the door? She had to stop thinking that way. Lizzy was safe with Connor and Caleb there. They wouldn't let her out of their sight. She was sure of that. Surer then she'd been of anything in her life. They loved her.

Her heart warmed when she went into the kitchen to make breakfast. Connor and Lizzy were at the table slurping bowls of cereal while they watched cartoons through the living room doorway.

When Gram had died, Lizzy was the only reason Jordan had to get out of bed in the mornings, the only reason she had to draw her next breath. She hadn't expected to add to her little family so quickly. At that moment, she felt content.

Caleb came in search of his first cup of coffee. Now that she'd gotten used to him, she hardly noticed his amazing resemblance to Connor.

"Uncle Cal!" Lizzy exclaimed. "I got to sleep with Mommy and Daddy last night."

"Good for you, sweetheart," he replied with a grin. The importance of his brother's new designation hadn't been lost on him.

Connor's smile grew with pride. She hoped it was the right thing to do, letting Lizzy call him Daddy.

Bobby Ray would never hold that title for Lizzy. Knowing that, a little piece of his presence in their lives dissolved.

She decided to carry her coffee out to the barn. Now that it had been repaired, she'd started thinking about what they could use it for. Large animals didn't appeal to her. If Connor was going to live here permanently, perhaps he could use the space as a workshop or something. He approached. It would be a good time to discuss it with him.

As he came closer she noticed stiffness in his gait. His dark expression caused concern.

"Where's Lizzy?"

"She's in the house with Cal. She's fine," Connor informed her. "I wanted to tell you what I just saw on a news report without her overhearing and asking questions."

"Have they found Bobby Ray?"

"No, they found Bennett, his attorney, dead in his car at the beach in Ft. Myers. They're sure it was a suicide. I can't help but wonder if it had something to do with the outcome of the court case."

"It seems strange for me to even think this," she replied, "but I feel bad for him. Suicide is a horrible act of desperation. The man must have had redeeming qualities at some time during his life, no matter what kind of worm he became later. He may have even had a family."

"That's why I love you so much." Connor kissed the top of her head as he hugged her. "You're struggling to find something nice to say about the guy. That's damn generous of you, considering he tried to help Butler take your daughter a week ago."

"You have to forgive people or it eats at your soul."

"Do you forgive Butler? Do you honestly think I should?"

"That's a whole lot harder. We're still dealing with him. Someday, maybe we can put it behind us. I can't say that I hate him. Hate is too hard to live with. But that doesn't mean I won't do anything I have to, to protect my family."

They entered the house to find John sitting in the living room with Caleb. Both men looked up with serious expressions. A chill ran up her spine.

"Where's Lizzy?" she inquired for the second time.

"I sent her to her room to play for a while," Caleb told her. "There's been another development."

"What's going on?" Connor asked.

John stood to pace while he thought about how to tell them what he had learned. He hadn't finished telling the story to Caleb, but he started over from the beginning. "You know, I have contacts with the police department back home. I had asked one of my friends to give me a run-down on the woman who'd picked Butler up from the prison."

Connor interrupted, "Yeah, the hooker, Doris something, right?"

"Right, well, her name just came up again. My friend remembered me asking about her, so he called me this morning. It seems her body was found in Bradford County, not far from the prison. Some teenagers were four-wheeling out on a service road and came across her remains in a stand of trees. It was pretty disgusting Jordan, you don't have to hear this."

"No, go on. I need to know what we're up against.

This obviously involves Bobby Ray." Jordan suddenly felt cold and leaned against Connor.

"She suffered massive head trauma. The rest is hard to say. She's been dead for a while. They're guessing she was killed just after he left the prison. They found a large rock with traces on it near her head. Her clothes were scattered in the brushes by the road." John took a deep breath. "They also found a man's shirt close to her body. In the pocket was a note with your name and address on it, Jordan. Their pretty sure it was the one Butler left the prison wearing."

Connor stood and headed for the phone. "There may be more evidence in the car. It's still at the police impound lot."

"One more thing, Connor." John looked at him, and then Caleb. "My friend didn't have a number to reach me. He left a message at the office."

"Do you know who he talked to?" Caleb asked.

"Does it matter?" John smirked. "Everything goes across the old man's desk."

"We'll deal with that later if we have to." Connor called information for the number of the Ft. Myers police department.

"He got away from us during the party, Saturday," John said to Caleb. "But we plan to find that son of a bitch again."

"You and Ted had better just watch your asses. This guy is getting crazier by the day."

****

Bobby Ray sat at the end of the bar where it curled around and tucked into a dark corner near the door. He kept his head down, his face covered by the shadow of a baseball cap. No one in Mayville knew what he looked like except the people who'd been in the courtroom in Ft. Myers. No pictures had appeared with the short article in the local paper. Still, it was a risk coming here. The way he figured though, the cops wouldn't expect him to be so close.

He'd blow town tonight, but first he wanted to hear the gossip. He didn't have Bennett to take care of that anymore, the stupid fuck.

The story of Bennett's suicide was on the front page of the Ft. Myers paper. He'd finally gotten his fifteen minutes of fame. Bobby Ray had placed the paper in front of him on the bar, but it wasn't getting any attention. He'd thought it would set tongues wagging, but it had been a bust. Instead, the bartender talked to the handful of customers about the high school football team's chances of making the play-offs in the coming season.

Bobby Ray laid ten dollars on the bar to pay for the two beers he'd drank, figuring he may as well leave. As he was about to stand, the door opened. Jackpot! It was two of the people who'd been at Jordan's house the night he carved up the cat.

The old man and the flashy blonde bimbo sat at a table in the back. He waited for them to order their drinks before moving to a dartboard nearby. It was closer and quieter than one of the pool tables. He'd be able to hear their conversation even if anyone else decided to play.

"Do you want to tell me what's on your mind?" the bimbo asked.

"It's nothing."

"Have I done something wrong?"

Maybe it has something to do with your fashion

choices. Bobby Ray chuckled quietly.

"No, I think I have… I've been thinking, ever since the party at Jordan's house. All those young people were running around and having fun, and there you sat, tied to an old goat like me."

"You know I don't think of you that way. We've had a lot of fun together."

Surprise, surprise, they're knocking boots.

"It's been a lot of years, Joyce. Why'd you do it? You knew there wasn't any future with me."

"Did you see the doctor again?" Joyce asked. "Have there been any new developments?"

"What developments are you expecting? I explained to you before, I'm not going to get any better. Why waste your youth this way? Why spend time with a dying man. You should be out having fun and finding someone to spend the rest of your life with. I never should have started anything with you, knowing that I wasn't going to be able to see it through"

Could the old guy get any more pathetic? So he was dying, aren't we all?

"Fifteen years ago you weren't dying," she reminded him. "And, who else would take a second look at a crazy hair stylist who lives with her mother? I knew from the beginning that you'd never feel the same about me, as you did Ms. Holbrook. She was a great lady.

"I'm the one who was selfish. I should have made you tell her how you felt, right from the start. I don't have a life. I own a business that takes every minute of my day. Then, I take care of my mom all night. I sneak away maybe once a week to keep you company. You've been a good friend, Arnie."

So their names are Joyce and Arnie...and they are equally pathetic.

"Well, I'm going to try to be a better friend," Arnie stated. "I don't want you to do this anymore. I want you to start going out and looking for someone you can hang on to. I'm serious, Joyce, I don't want you to come around anymore."

"You don't mean that, Arnie."

"Yes, I do."

Good old Arnie took off and left Joyce, the bimbo, sitting alone in a bar. Classy. Bobby Ray stepped to the pool table. Now was a good time to be noticed. The woman felt vulnerable and in need of affection. It wasn't beyond him to take advantage of an opportunity.

But then the waitress ran over squealing like a pig at feeding time. "Joyce! We haven't seen you in here in a coon's age. I was just telling my sister today that I needed to call you for an appointment. My roots are grown out so badly, I look like a skunk pulled wrong side out."

"I've got some time at two tomorrow, but for now, how about a light beer?" She looked at the bar again. "It sure is slow in here tonight."

"Yeah, but that cutie at the dart board is keeping me busy just watching him." Allison pointed behind her. "You should go over there. He's been playing solo for over an hour. I bet he could use some company."

Okay, he'd been noticed by the wrong person, but that didn't mean he couldn't play. When Joyce looked around at him, he plastered on a big smile for her, like he'd have anything to do with the sleazy skank.

"Hi," he said. "Haven't I seen you around town?"

"I've lived here all my life, you may have. I don't

remember seeing you before, though. I think I would have remembered."

"You can call me Al." He sauntered over, knowing he must look good to her after the old man she'd been with. "What's your name?"

"I'm Joyce. I own the beauty salon here in town."

"Oh, a businesswoman, I see." He poured on the charm and flattery. "This must be my lucky night. I'm new in town. Maybe you could show me around a few of the hot spots."

"There are no hot spots in Mayville, honey. This is it."

"Then why don't we go to the diner for a cup of coffee?"

A look of alarm knit her brows. Had he gone too far?

"I really can't, I just stopped by to wait for friends. We're going to a movie tonight."

"A night out with the girls?"

"My friend and her fiancé are setting me up with his brother. It's kind of a double date."

In your dreams, bitch. Who did she think she was fooling?

"Tell your friend hello for me. As a matter of fact, you could give her a note." He picked up the cocktail napkin from her table, pulled a pen from his shirt pocket, and scribbled a single word. He folded the napkin back to the way it had been and placed it on the table.

He knew she'd think he was discreetly giving her his phone number. He wished he could see her face when she read that one word, *Meow*.

****

Connor hung up the phone and turned to Jordan.

"Joyce is stranded at the bar in town. I'm going to get her car started and follow her home. I'll be back soon. Lock the doors while I'm gone and set the alarm."

Chapter Nineteen

On Tuesday morning Jordan went downstairs to make breakfast. She saw Connor through the window, sorting the mail by the roadside box. It had been a long night. She'd had a lot of trouble sleeping, since the incident with poor little Tom. The information about Doris Pritchett had given her a few nightmares too. She jumped when the phone rang.

"Hello?"

"Hello, this is Ian McCrae. I called to find out just what the hell is going on down there."

"This is who?"

"McCrae, Ian McCrae. I know you know who I am. You have both of my sons, mixed up in all kinds of trouble. I don't know why I was kept out of the loop on this case, but I'm damned well going to be involved now. I've spoken to my investigators already this morning. I don't like what I'm hearing. I don't know what kind of game you're playing, but I know it's dangerous. My boys are lawyers, not cops, not soldiers, not bodyguards. I want them back in this office immediately, and I mean both of them."

"Look, Mr. McCrae, I'm sorry I've caused trouble for your sons. That wasn't my intention." Jordan hadn't noticed that Connor had walked into the room. "Please let me try to explain."

Connor slammed the envelopes on the table and

pushed the speaker button on the phone's base. "Dad, this is Connor. Jordan has nothing to explain to you. I'm here because I want to be. No one is holding Caleb hostage either. You have no idea what this woman has been through. The last thing she needs is you calling her at this time of the morning to rake her over the coals. I won't put up with it."

"What do you mean, you won't put up with it? I'll do as I damn well please. You boys are in way over your heads. I want you both back in Tampa today."

"That's not going to happen, Dad. This is my home now and I'm not leaving my family unprotected. You don't know much about me, if that's the kind of man you think I am. She's going to be my wife. You'll show her more respect than this if you ever expect to hear from me again."

"Are you serious? You finally decide to settle down and you find a woman with a psychopathic ex-husband? We've already been through hell with you, and then we had to deal with Caleb's problems, now this. You two boys are going to be the death of your mother and me."

"Maybe you just need to stop thinking of us as boys. We're both thirty-five years old." Connor ran his hand through his hair and took a deep breath. "I know Caleb has problems, but I figure he'll tell me about them when he's ready. I respect him enough not to interfere. I demand the same respect from you."

"You could give us a hell of a lot more respect too, son. I'm still a partner in this practice. I expect a full report by the end of the day. I also expect you to call your mother and let her know you're getting married. What the hell are you thinking, not telling her a thing like that? We haven't even met the girl yet." Ian cleared his throat and softened his voice. "Is Jordan still listening?"

Connor turned to her and shrugged. She could tell he was still angry. "I'm still here, Mr. McCrae."

"Jordan, I'm sorry I lost my temper with you. I should have asked for one of my b...sons instead of unloading on you that way. I worry about them. Would you please make sure Connor calls his mother today?"

"Yes sir, I'll do that. I'm sorry for getting them involved in this mess."

"Well, we'll find some way out of it. Goodbye, Jordan."

"Goodbye, Mr. McCrae." After hanging up the phone she looked up at Connor. "Well, I guess I've made a great first impression on him."

"He's just jealous that he can't be here to share in all the excitement," Connor replied. "I'm sorry he acted like a jack-ass. You handled him well."

"Are you going to call your mother?"

"Yeah, he was right about that. I'll take care of it." He paused for a moment. "He did confirm one thing for me. I've had a feeling Cal has something troubling on his mind. I don't know what it could be, but it must be serious. We shared everything, until six years ago. It's my fault he doesn't feel like he can confide in me now. I hope we can get that back."

****

Bobby Ray sat up on the side of the bed. He looked around at the sleazy hotel room. He'd been stuck inside for days. It was time to look for the next hole-in-the-wall to hide in. He could afford better. He still had a lot of Nita's money, but he needed a place where people didn't look too closely.

In the shower he thought about Nita. He was starting to miss her. She was only a whore, but she was fun. If things had started to go wrong he'd planned for her to lure the kid away. She was gone by the time he needed her help. He really didn't want the kid, but she was the best way to get under Jordan's skin.

Thinking about Nita and Jordan made him horny. He wished he could have talked the bimbo into leaving with him the night before. She was older than he liked, but she would have scratched his itch. It would have been cool to drop her on Jordan's doorstep after he was finished with her. Maybe he would give that more thought. He needed a woman soon, though.

He looked at himself in the mirror. His hair and beard were growing in nicely. Soon he could walk around Mayville unnoticed.

Bobby Ray pulled a bottle of water from the little refrigerator, before he sat on the end of the bed and turned on the TV. The news was on the only channel that came in clearly. He packed his clothes while they talked about the weather and traffic. He was putting together the scattered sketches on the dresser top, when he heard his name. Turning around, he saw his picture, full screen, on the TV. This was going to complicate things.

Next, they showed the place in the trees where he had left Doris. An old picture of her was displayed in the top right corner of the screen. The roaring in his head kept him from hearing what they were saying. How had they found her? How did they know it was him? He shouldn't have kept her damned car for so long. He cleared his mind in time to hear the reporter's last few comments.

"Bobby Ray Butler is still believed to be in the state of Florida. He was last seen in the Ft. Myers area. At that time, he was driving a late model, red Honda Civic with extreme body damage. If anyone sees this man, you are asked to contact the nearest law enforcement agency. Under no circumstances should you approach him. He's considered extremely dangerous."

Bobby Ray drove for nearly an hour until he reached a state park near Lake Okeechobee. He left the car on the side of a small dirt road and walked through the woods. The temperature was near triple-digits; he hoped this wouldn't take long.

Finally he came across a man fishing at the edge of a canal. His small tent was a few feet from Bobby Ray's hiding place. His pick-up truck was at the top of the embankment. Bobby Ray quietly made his way to the tent. By the campfire was a knife still dirty from cleaning fish. He picked it up and approached the man from behind. The fisherman reared up as Bobby Ray circled his head with his left arm. With the dirty knife, Bobby Ray quickly slit his throat. He hadn't had a chance to utter a sound. The bleeding man kicked and clawed before losing consciousness.

Bobby Ray dug through the fisherman's pockets for his keys. Before he left, he took the Miami Dolphins baseball cap and sunglasses that had fallen on the ground. He found a first-aid kit in the truck that had a bottle of rubbing alcohol. He gathered some of the man's camping gear he thought he might need. The small propane stove and cooler might come in handy. Before he left, he shoved the man's body into the canal.

The gators would finish cleaning up the mess.

****

"Did you ever call your mother?" Jordan asked.

"I sure did," Connor replied as he drove her home from work. "It scared her to death. I normally call on Christmas, Mother's Day, and her birthday. I was off schedule."

"How did she take the news?"

"She was happy. I told her all about you and Lizzy. She can't wait to meet you both."

"Then you obviously didn't tell her everything." Jordan gazed out the window to hide her concern.

"Let's just take this one step at a time. Hopefully, it will be over before she has to find out the details."

"Did you talk to Cal?"

"Yep, all day long. We're thinking about building one of those wooden play sets for Lizzy."

"You know what I mean."

"When he feels like talking to me, he will. And, I'll be there to listen." Connor hesitated. "I need to tell you about something that happened Sunday night."

Jordan listened intently as Connor relayed the events in the bar as Joyce had explained them to him.

"I wish I had never come back here," she said. "I've put everyone I love in danger. And, I have an awful feeling this is going to get worse."

"I don't agree. You have a lot of people here who are looking out for you and Lizzy. Besides that, if you hadn't come back here, we wouldn't have met. You'd be alone to face this asshole. I hate to think how this would have ended." Conner took her hand and brought it to his lips, kissing her knuckles lightly. "I don't ever want to hear you talk that way. You've given me more

168

than I've ever dreamed of having. No one is going to take you away from me."

"But look at the way we're living, Connor. Lizzy can't go to preschool. I can't go to the store alone. The house is like a prison. None of us are sleeping at night. You and I have just gotten engaged and we hardly make love anymore. We're too busy listening for strange noises or watching out the windows. I feel like this is pulling us apart."

"I'm sorry, Jordan. I promise this will be over soon. I feel like I have to do this. If I can't protect you, then I don't deserve you. I'm sorry I haven't been more attentive. I guess I just figured we'd have a lifetime to love each other once this was over."

"I guess you're right. I'm just on my last nerve. Every time I turn around, Bobby Ray rears his ugly head and we're back to square one."

"No honey, we're getting closer to ending this every day. Just try to be patient." Connor watched the road as he thought about Ted and John going home soon, leaving them to find Butler on their own. Ted was married last year and had a pregnant wife to get back to. John had a wife and a seventeen-year-old son at home. Connor couldn't ask them to stay any longer.

Connor and Jordan picked up their nightly routine as if the discussion had never happened. They did their best to make life as normal as possible for Lizzy, but even she was feeling a bit restless. After she'd gone to bed, they watched the news on TV. No progress had been reported on the manhunt for Bobby Ray. The lead story of the day was a search for a man who'd been reported missing when he didn't return from a camping trip the previous day.

Chapter Twenty

Jordan was surprised to find Lizzy still in bed after she'd dressed for work the next day.

"Don't you feel well, honey?" she asked as she knelt beside the bed.

"Why do I have to get up? I don't have anything to do. I miss playing at Mrs. Rogers's house. All my friends are there."

"Don't you like to stay with Uncle Cal and Daddy?" It still felt strange to refer to Connor that way.

"They try real hard, but I think they're running out of ideas."

"I'm afraid they're going to miss having breakfast with you," Jordan coaxed.

"Okay. I'll get up."

Jordan went down to the kitchen and told the men about her talk with Lizzy while the men shared the newspaper.

"This is just what I've been looking for." Caleb held up a sale paper for a local hardware store. "If this doesn't help, nothing will." He pointed to a playground kit on sale. "We could borrow Coleman's truck and pick one up today. I think it'd be perfect at the north end of the lawn."

"I've got an idea too," Connor said. "There's a carnival going on just a few miles away. We can go as soon as you get out of work today, Jordan. You'd have time to change clothes and I'll have dinner ready."

Lizzy stood at the door looking like she'd just found Santa under her Christmas tree. She ran across the room and threw herself into her new daddy's arms, hugging him as hard as she could.

"I guess he wins," Caleb chuckled "I'd better get you to work. He can't possibly drive with that monkey around his neck. I have a feeling she won't let go for a while."

The carnival wasn't as crowded on a Thursday night as Jordan had feared it would be. They enjoyed walking in the evening breeze, listening to the sounds of tinny music, pinging game machines, and boisterous barkers. The bright lights and sweet greasy food smells took their minds off their usual train of thought. The grown-ups watched Lizzy ride the carousel and feed the baby lambs. She ate cotton candy and played the ring toss. Connor and Caleb competed in winning her the biggest prizes.

When the evening wound down, Caleb took Lizzy from Connor's shoulders.

"Why don't you two lovebirds take a turn on the Ferris wheel while Lizzy and I check out the face painting booth?"

"I want to make a suggestion," Connor said to Jordan while they waited for more riders from the top of the ride. "But, I know you're going to throw a fit. It's been such a great evening that I hate to ruin it. If you get mad at me, do you promise to leave it on this Ferris wheel?"

"I hate when a conversation starts out like this. Okay, I promise. What's on your mind?"

"I want you to think about taking some time off

from your job. You know as well as I do that we don't need the money. It's getting harder to keep Lizzy entertained, and you have more experience with that than Cal or I put together. Also, it's going to get harder to keep you both safe after Ted and John leave. Charlie would understand. Would you think about it?"

"I guess it would be better if we stuck together. I hate to bail on Charlie, though. Let me talk to him tomorrow. I'll miss getting out of the house and being around people, but I guess that's what you and Cal have been doing for a while now. It's a fair suggestion. I can't expect the two of you to stay at home with my daughter while I go out every day."

"It's not like that, Jordan. She's our daughter now. I'd live closed up in a cave with her if that's what it took.

"I'm starting to wonder what Cal's motives are though. He never takes his eyes off her. I knew he'd love her, but he seems almost obsessed with protecting her. It's not like him to be away from the office this long. He's always been a workaholic."

The ride came to a stop.

"Speaking of Cal and Lizzy, I guess we'd better get over to the face painting booth. It's getting late," Jordan said. "We should head back to the house."

"Yeah, let's see what they've turned our little monkey into."

As they walked toward the three-sided shelter Caleb had headed for, Connor's expression grew dark. He walked more quickly and stretched to peer over people's heads in front of him. Jordan could almost feel his pulse quicken as he led her along the path. She didn't ask questions, but hurried to keep pace with him.

She was developing a feeling of panic from his sudden change of behavior.

"Something is wrong, I can feel it. Cal's in trouble."

They found Lizzy sitting on a stool inside the booth. The clown smile painted around her lips did nothing to hide the worry in her eyes.

"I don't know where Uncle Cal went," she groaned when they reached her. "He was right over there, and then he was gone." She pointed to the side of the booth to her right.

"Stay with her and don't leave this booth," Connor demanded in a stern voice. He headed in the direction Lizzy had pointed. Jordan was torn between keeping Lizzy safe in the tent and following Connor.

****

Connor found his brother only a few feet off the path between the booth he'd taken Lizzy to and the next one. He was laying facedown across the cables that ran along the ground. A broken board had been left beside him. He'd been struck across the left side of his head. He was bleeding.

As Connor turned him over, Cal moaned and reached up to feel the gash swelling on his head. With his eyes still closed, he spoke only one word. "Lizzy..."

"Lizzy's fine. We need to get you to a doctor. What happened?"

"Hell if I know," Caleb groaned. "I was watching Lizzy, and then the lights went out. Now, my head hurts like crazy."

"Maybe somebody was after your wallet."

"The surprise is on them," Caleb grimaced. "I never carry a wallet in a place like this. My money is in the front pocket of my jeans. I guess there's a pretty disappointed mugger somewhere around here. Are you sure Lizzy's okay?"

"Yeah, she's fine, but you could use a few stitches. Let's get the girls out of here." Connor pulled off his shirt to staunch the bleeding.

The hospital was close by, but the ride seemed to take forever. Inside the emergency room, Caleb was taken straight to x-ray. Connor took care of the paperwork.

"Thank God it wasn't Bobby Ray," Jordan remarked. "We'd have known it if it had been. He'd have left something to take credit for catching us with our guard down."

"I think it was a mugger, like Cal said," Connor agreed. "We got lucky this time. From now on, we stick together. Dammit, this was my fault."

"I wonder if that's what Cal said when you got hurt. You know you guys aren't super heroes. Sometimes things happen that we don't have control over. This was the fault of the man who hit him, not you."

A doctor came out of the double doors and walked to the corner where they were waiting, his long white lab coat swishing around his thighs. They were relieved to see a smile on his face.

"That brother of yours has a hard head. He does have a slight concussion, though, so we'd like to keep him overnight for observation."

"Can I see him before we go?" Connor asked.

"Sure, but only you," the doctor insisted. "They just started stitching him up."

Connor walked into the room the doctor had

indicated. A paper shield covered Caleb's head with a hole over the injury. Connor winced when he saw the needle sink into his brother's skin.

"Well Cal, it looks like you're still going to be as pretty as ever after the hair grows back in that spot."

"I guess you're pretty glad it was me and not you." Caleb laughed.

"Why would you say something like that?"

"Because, I don't mind getting a hair cut once in a while. You'd be going apeshit on these poor nurses."

Connor let out a laugh. "I'm going to take Jordan and Lizzy home. I'll be back in the morning to pick you up. Try to stay out of trouble, okay?"

"Okay Con. You be careful too, and watch out for our girls."

The nurse tied off the last suture and removed the shield. Connor stood by the door with a grave expression.

"You know I'd shave my head if it meant keeping you out of harm's way, Cal."

"I know bro, me too."

Connor turned and walked away.

****

Jordan set the security alarm then led the way upstairs as Lizzy slept on Connor's shoulder. She was glad that she'd washed the grease paint off her face at the hospital. She removed Lizzy's shoes after she'd been laid in her bed, but decided to let her sleep in her clothes. It had been a long night. The morning would be soon enough for her to take a bath and change.

Connor was already in the shower when she left Lizzy's room. She hesitated in the hallway for a moment before walking into the bathroom. Stripping away her clothes she joined him under the steamy water. He was just rinsing the shampoo from his hair, letting the lather slide down his muscular body to the floor of the tub.

"I knew I'd get you in here with me sooner or later," he said as he soaped a sponge. He wrapped his arms around her and ran the sponge up and down her back.

Jordan leaned her head into his shoulder as the water cascaded over them both. She hadn't realized how tense she'd been until her muscles began to relax.

"I've never done this before," she murmured. "I mean, showered with anyone."

"Let me show you how it's done." After a long warm kiss, he stepped back just enough to rub the sudsy sponge over the rest of her body. She took the sponge from his hand and began washing him while he shampooed her hair.

"I could get used to this. As a matter-of-fact, it could become a habit."

"That's what I'm hoping." He kissed her again.

She was disappointed when he turned off the water. "Let's save the rest of this lesson for the next time. It's been a long night and I need to lie down." He wrapped a large bath sheet around her and led her by the hand to the bedroom.

"You're a tease, Mr. McCrae."

"Who said I was lying down to sleep? I'm not finished with you yet."

"Are you sure the house is secure? Maybe I should check on Lizzy."

"The doors are bolted. The windows are locked. You set the security alarm yourself. But, I have a surprise for you." Connor opened the drawer in the bedside table and brought out a white electronic device. A green light glowed below its speaker.

"Is that what I think it is?"

"Yep." He grinned. "It's a baby monitor. I picked it up at the store while we were out today. We can hear her, but she can't hear us."

He removed the towel from around her and threw it on the floor before sitting on the bed and pulling her onto his lap. She lazily lay against him as he ran his hands across her shoulders and down to her breasts. He lingered there, to tease her nipples, his erection stirring for attention. One hand came down to slide between her legs. She was more than ready for him.

"You take over from here, baby," he whispered over her shoulder as he passed her a condom.

This time when they made love their actions were more physical than emotional, more urgent and varied. She had a need to work out the tension of the last few hours. Jordan was amazed at the way their minds and bodies synchronized to accomplish mutual waves of excitement, ecstasy, satisfaction.

Connor rolled onto his side, his arms still wrapped around her. They slept better than they had in weeks.

The next morning they woke together feeling well rested. They stretched lazily as the morning sun washed over them through the window. A tap on their door alerted them both to the fact they were totally naked. They scrambled out of bed to find clothes. Thankfully they'd had the presence of mind to lock the door the night before.

Lizzy bounced into the room as soon as the door opened. "I'm hungry. When are you guys going to come make breakfast? Your bed sure does get messy. The covers are all on the floor."

"You need a bath before you do anything else," Jordan told her. "Those clothes are filthy."

"Well, okay, but do I have to wash off my tattoo?"

"What tattoo?"

"The one the man gave me at the carnival. After Uncle Cal left, he said a tattoo would make me feel better. He said you'd like it too, Mommy. He said it was a surprise for you. He did it with a marker like the ones I have. Are you surprised?"

"Show me your tattoo, Lizzy."

Lizzy proudly lifted her sleeve to reveal the outline of a cross on her shoulder. Jordan could barely breathe. The drawing on her daughter's shoulder was almost an exact replica of the tattoo Bobby Ray wore. He'd touched Lizzy, spoken to her. He'd practically been alone with her while she and Connor rode on a Ferris wheel. He could have killed Caleb. Images ran through her mind of all he could have done to Lizzy. Jordan wanted to throw up.

"I'll call the police." Connor eased her back to the bed.

Chapter Twenty-One

After Lizzy's bath, she ate a bowl of cereal. Jordan and Connor quietly sat across the table sipping their coffee.

"Can I have the picture you took, Daddy?"

"No Lizzy, I have to give it to the police. They're going to be here soon to ask you some questions."

"You took a picture of it?" Jordan exclaimed.

"Yes, I did. I couldn't expect Lizzy to wear the evidence on her arm."

Jordan ran from the room and up the stairs. Her bedroom door slammed a few seconds later.

"Why is Mommy mad? Did I do something bad?"

"She's not mad, monkey, she's just upset. The man that drew the tattoo on your arm was the bad man. The one the police have been looking for."

"He's the man who killed my Tom?"

Connor nodded as he wiped a drop of milk from her chin.

"I'm sorry," she whined. "I didn't mean to talk to a stranger, but I didn't know where any of you were. I was really scared."

"I know, sweetheart. I'm sorry the whole thing happened. But, now you know what he looks like. Do you think you can remember if you see him again?"

"Yes, I think so."

"That's my girl. Now go up to your room and try to

remember everything he said so you can tell the policemen. I'm going to call Uncle Cal at the hospital and see how he's doing."

Lizzy left the room with her head down. Connor wished so badly this was over. The tension was getting to all of them.

Normally, Lizzy would still be talking about the carnival, laughing and happy. Jordan would be basking in the afterglow of lovemaking. He missed her sexy, secret smiles. Would they ever be that carefree again?

When the doorbell rang, he opened it to find two plain clothes police detectives, one male and one female. After introductions, Connor and Jordan agreed to allow the female, Detective Shannon, to take Lizzy for a walk around the yard. The male, Detective Tucker, seemed anxious to talk to them privately.

"Have you found out anything new, Detective?" Connor asked.

"We haven't found Butler, but we did find the car. It was three counties away in a wooded area of a public park. It would have taken us forever to find it if they hadn't been conducting a search in that area for a missing camper."

"Did they find the camper?"

"No, not a sign of him. Have you noticed any strange vehicles lately?"

"No, but we were mainly looking out for the red Honda."

"He had to have had another vehicle to get back from the park. There's no doubt in our minds that Butler was the man who spoke to Lizzy last night. We're just trying to determine if he said anything to her that may give away his hiding place. A current description is good, too.

"We're going to have a patrol car pass your house frequently. Don't let it alarm you. Also we need your brother to make a statement. Tomorrow will be soon enough. I know he doesn't have much to tell us, but we still need it on record." He turned to Jordan. "Is there anything you can tell me about Butler that I don't already know? Any habits, phobias, or fetishes? I hate to ask, but we need to get this guy off the streets."

She hung her head and thought for several minutes. Connor sensed her discomfort. He stood and walked toward the kitchen. "I'm going to make some fresh coffee."

After he'd left the room, Jordan spoke. "He hates homosexuals and prostitutes. He has a fear of diseases, especially STDs. If any kind of bodily fluid touches his skin, he goes crazy. He has a way with women. He likes young pretty girls. The innocent types who don't seem promiscuous are his favorite. He'll target a woman who seems lonely and shy. He charms and flatters them into trusting him. At first, he seems too good to be true. Before you know what's happening, you're trapped. You're too ashamed and embarrassed to complain. My first time was on my wedding night. I was so stupid. He convinced me that it was a wife's duty to fulfill her husband's every fantasy. The next morning I had to scrub blood off the wall. He said it would never happen again, but that was just the beginning. I think he may be worse now." She gave a shy smile. "I'm sorry. I don't think this was the information you were looking for. I guess I just got carried away. I've been remembering a lot about him lately."

Connor pushed himself away from the other side of

the doorframe where he had been listening. His hands shook as he ran water into the coffee carafe. Detective Tucker came up behind him and took it from his hand.

"She's gone upstairs to rest for a while. I'll finish the coffee. Maybe you should get some air."

"You knew I was listening?" Connor asked.

"I know I would have if it was the woman I loved."

Connor walked out to the front porch and found John sitting in the rocking chair by the living room window.

"How long have you been here?"

"Long enough."

"You heard everything too then?"

"Yep."

"I'm sorry you had to hear that. I guess it brought back some unwanted memories for you."

"I'm sorry you had to hear it too," John replied. "If anyone knows how bad it hurts when someone you love has been treated that way, it's me. Beth would have been twenty years old this year. It's hard to believe she's been gone four years now. I think, if she'd survived her attacker, I'd just concentrate on making sure she was happy and letting her know how much I loved her. Nothing else matters as much as that."

"I know you're right John, but I have one other thing to do first. I have to make her safe. That won't happen until Butler is history. We've got a lot of people looking now, and enough evidence to put him on death row. I think it's about time for you to get back home. You have a family waiting for you."

"I was hoping you'd be coming back too, after all this was over. Now I see that you've made a home here. I'm happy for you, Connor. If anybody deserves it, it's you. I hope you'll both be as content as Laura and I have been.

"Even Josh is starting to straighten up. He took Beth's death harder than we'd expected, but I think he's finally coming to terms with it. He's given up the black lipstick and eyeliner. Maybe some of that jewelry in his face will be gone by the time I get back."

"Well, good luck with that, John, seriously. I sure appreciate all you've done for us. If you need anything, you just call. We'll send a wedding invitation as soon as we can."

"I'll look forward to it." John stood to shake Connor's hand.

John walked to his car and drove away. He had been employed by the firm for twenty years, but more than that, he'd become a member of the family. They'd been through an awful lot in all that time. The only time Connor had come close to Tampa since the attack was to visit with John and his family. It was the day after their daughter had been buried near their home in Brandon. He remembered how it felt to see the whole family so devastated. He couldn't let that happen here.

He watched Lizzy walk toward the house, holding Detective Shannon's hand. He was glad the police had thought to send someone who could relate to a child in an unthreatening manner.

Lizzy's little freckled face looked up at him smiling, auburn braids over each shoulder. He pictured Jordan, twenty-five years ago, looking exactly that way. The tension eased from his shoulders. "Why don't you go upstairs and color a picture for your new friend, while the grown-ups talk for a while," he suggested.

"Okay! I'll make a picture of my room, and I'll put

you in it, too."

"Did you find out anything?" Tucker asked, as soon as Lizzy's bedroom door closed.

"Mostly what we expected," Detective Shannon informed him. "His beard and hair are a little longer now. He pretended to work at the carnival. No clue as to his whereabouts, though.

"The kid was pretty specific. She has a great memory. She even told me what color his shoelaces were. There was only one thing that stood out. He was wearing an old Miami Dolphins baseball cap."

"That's not good," Tucker replied.

"Why?" Connor asked. "You can pick up a Dolphins cap in a million places down here."

"This one was old and frayed, like the one our missing camper was wearing when he was last seen," Shannon said. "We'd better put out an APB on the missing truck. I've got a bad feeling it's more than a coincidence Butler's car was found in that area."

Caleb arrived an hour later in a cab to prevent inconveniencing anyone. His head was wrapped in a large bandage. He went straight to his room with Connor close behind. "Help me get this thing off, Con. My head is sweating and it makes the stitches burn like hell. I need a shower."

"You're in a good mood. I don't suppose they sent you home with any drugs. I'd kind of hate to have to knock you out again."

"They didn't let me sleep at all last night. Then, I had to get through a pile of paperwork to come home. In the meantime, the cops showed up and told me about what happened to Lizzy. The doctor gave me a prescription for Percocet. Those things make me nauseous. I can't believe I was so stupid last night. She could have been taken right out from under my nose. I'm so sorry, Connor. It was my fault." Caleb sat on the end of his bed and dropped his face into his hands.

"It wasn't your fault, Cal." Connor put his hand on his brother's shoulder. "You're going to find this hard to believe, but I was told last night that we aren't super heroes."

"Who says so?" Cal grinned.

"Jordan."

"Then Jordan doesn't hate my guts?" Caleb groaned.

"Not yet. She really hasn't gotten to know you well, though. If you don't get some sleep, we're all going to hate you." Connor turned around to leave.

"Hey Connor. I just have one question. When Jordan told you that you weren't a super hero, you weren't doing anything intimate, were you?"

"No, but when you hear her screaming, *take me Captain Amazing*, you should stand as far away from the door as possible. The sonic percussions may hurt your head." He ducked as a pillow flew over his head.

Connor was still laughing when he turned to find Jordan standing a few feet away, arms crossed over her chest and toe tapping.

"It's time to take out the garbage, Captain Amazing."

Chapter Twenty-Two

In the wee hours of Saturday morning Connor was snuggled against Jordan's warm, naked body. It took a few rings for the phone to wake him. "Hello," he growled sleepily.

"Boss? It's Ted. I'm sorry to wake you."

"What's up, man? Is Jenny in labor? Has the baby come? Did you get home in time?" Connor sat up and rubbed the sleep from his eyes.

"No, I'm still at the hotel. The baby isn't due for six more weeks."

"Why haven't you gone home yet? I thought you were leaving yesterday."

"So did I, but John talked me into waiting another day. Last night, at about eight, he had an idea. He took the rental car and said he'd be back in two hours. I've been trying his cell phone since eleven. It's three o'clock now. I'm stranded in this stupid hotel room. I was really hoping you knew where he is."

"He didn't say where he was going?" Connor was more awake now.

"No, but he was wearing jeans and carrying his handgun. He's been all wound up since he left your house yesterday."

"Pack up and leave a message for him at the front desk. I have to get dressed before I pick you up. We'll put on a pot of coffee and try to figure this out."

Jordan was stirring as he hung up the phone. He heard an urgent tapping on the door. "Connor, open up," Caleb insisted in a loud whisper.

Connor was off the bed and to the door in a few long strides.

Jordan grabbed the sheet higher as Caleb came in wearing only boxer shorts. He didn't seem fazed at all that Connor stood before him totally naked. He walked right past him to grab Jordan's robe and tossed it to her. "Get this on and go to Lizzy. Keep her in there. I don't want either of you to leave her room until we come back to get you."

Jordan pulled on the robe. Caleb's face was tear-stained and he held his hand against the large bandage on the side of his head. Something terrible had happened. Connor pulled on a pair of shorts.

"What's going on, Cal?"

Before Jordan could finish tying the belt on her robe, Caleb grabbed her by the arm and pulled her out of the bed.

"Get your hands off of her," Connor growled.

"I'm sorry. We have to hurry. He might still be alive." Caleb ran from the room and down the stairs.

Connor followed pushing the panic button on the alarm pad as he passed it. The police would be there within minutes. He didn't bother taking the steps out the back door, but jumped over them. He stopped short seeing Caleb under the oak tree. His arms were wrapped around John's legs in an attempt to hold him up.

"Help me get him down!" Caleb cried.

"Look at his face, Cal. He's already gone," Connor moaned as his own eyes filled with tears.

Ted arrived in a patrol car twenty minutes later. He answered Detective Tucker's questions and was finally able to reach Connor and Caleb where they sat at the kitchen table with Jordan. Over a white speaker before them, he heard Lizzy's soft breathing.

"You're sharper than any cop out here," Connor blurted. "Tell me what you saw out there."

"You two don't need to go running around like Rambo and Rocky. You need to let the cops handle this."

"Cut the crap, Ted. What do you see?" Caleb insisted.

"Okay," he said with a sigh. "You know when I got here the ground was still wet after a light rain from last night. The police cars were where they are now, no other tire tracks. No one has driven in from the front since yesterday. No one can get in from the back. Therefore, no vehicle was used. The heels of John's shoes caught a lot of grass. He was dragged. He was unconscious or dead already. He's too heavy to have been dragged far. While the grass was still wet, there was a path beaten down from that direction." He pointed toward the northeast corner just yards from the oak tree. "The bushes are broken there. Butler's not good at covering his tracks. He's not used to this kind of terrain. If he's still out there, he can be found. Now, who among these cops do I talk to? I'm playing this one by the book. It's too important to do otherwise."

"Okay, go get Detective Tucker," Connor told him. "He's the guy you were just talking to. He seems to be in charge."

"You're really going to turn this all over and sit back?" Caleb asked Connor.

188

"We're lawyers. We're not trained for this. But, we do know what happens if it's not handled correctly." Connors eyes panned the tree line through the window. "Besides that, we know he's close. He could be watching us now. If we leave Jordan and Lizzy here alone, it would be a perfect opportunity for him to come after them."

"How can you be so cool about this? When I got here I thought this guy was just a thug who robbed stores and beat women. He went way past that the day he got out of prison and killed the Pritchett woman." Anger had replaced the look of grief on Caleb's face.

"He was way past that, for me, before he even got out," Connor whispered.

"Why do you say that?"

"He was one of the men in the parking garage that night. He was the one with the knife."

Caleb sat in stunned silence for a moment. "How could you have kept something like that from me all this time?"

"I guess we all have our secrets, don't we, brother?"

"He only found out when he saw a picture I have of Bobby Ray." Jordan got up to refill their coffee mugs,

"It still would have been nice to know everything about who we're dealing with," Caleb groused.

Connor and Caleb were still glaring at each other when Ted returned with Detective Tucker.

"I had to call the old man," Ted announced. "I wanted him to be the one to tell Laura. He's on his way over there now. I imagine you'll hear from him soon."

"That's just what I need right now," Connor mumbled. "I'm already on his shit list."

"We'll all be expected to go back with John," Caleb said. "It's only right. He was here for us."

"Your man is being taken in to the medical examiner," Detective Tucker interrupted. "It shouldn't take long. You'll need to arrange transportation for him to be sent back to his family." He looked toward the trees as he continued. "I'm waiting for the trackers to arrive. They should be here any minute. These two guys are the best in south Florida. I'll keep everyone else back to follow them in. This will not be screwed up."

"We'll have to be out of town for a while," Connor said. "John was a close family friend. We'll have to pay our respects to his wife and son. Is that going to be a problem?"

"Actually, it will be a relief," Tucker replied. "Maybe the rest of us can get a little sleep while you're gone."

It was seven o'clock when the last police car left. Only a chosen few had stayed behind to search the woods. Connor and Caleb stood on the front porch watching them go. Both men were barefoot and only wore jeans.

"How am I going to explain the yellow tape in the back yard to Lizzy?" Connor asked. "I'll figure something out." Jordan offered. "I'm more concerned about facing your family."

"Wait until they get a look at your head." Connor pointed to Caleb's bandage.

"Oh, they've seen worse," Caleb reminded him.

A few hours later, Jordan stood in the middle of the kitchen with her hands on her hips.

"What do you mean we have to stay with your parents? I'll rent a hotel room."

"Sure, the security in those places is always great. Why not just sleep on a park bench? And, you can be the one to explain to my mother that we don't want to visit the family home."

"But I don't. Your father will eat me alive. Why can't we stay with Caleb?"

"I guess he sold his house a while back. He's living with our parents now."

"That settles it then, they don't have the room," Jordan smiled.

"Are you kidding? After six years away, I'll probably get lost in that place. It's huge."

Jordan narrowed her eyes at him. "I won't do it."

"Jordan, just listen to me for a minute. Can we really send John back without a word of comfort to his family after all he did for us?"

"No, of course not. We should be at the funeral."

"Am I supposed to just wave to my mother from across the room, after six years of being away? I've missed her, Jordan."

"No, you should see your mother. It's your father I'm afraid of." Jordan wrapped her arms around herself and shuddered.

Connor almost laughed at her dramatic gesture. "I know you're not going to like this idea, but I've been thinking about having you and Lizzy spend some time there. It would be the safest place she could be and leave me free to help search this monster out. Not to mention, they'll be your family soon too."

"I have to come back. If I'm not here, Bobby Ray won't have any reason to stick around. Then, there's no telling where he'll go. Besides that, what if your parents don't like me? Your dad already has a good start on that."

"If anybody can soften him up, you can. Look at what you've done for me. They'll just be grateful you got me out of that van." He gave her a little kiss on the forehead.

"I'm telling you now, the first sign of trouble and I'm out of there."

"It's a deal." Connor watched her walk away.

Caleb passed Jordan on her way out. "That was pretty smooth, brother. Do you really think you can hold the old man at bay?"

"It's me he'll be gunning for. I may be the first one out the door."

Chapter Twenty-Three

Bobby Ray was glad he'd had time to pack his truck before hanging the investigator in Jordan's tree. He was already on the road out of town when the first police car headed for her house. It had gone so smoothly. The guy just walked right into his trap. He'd been disappointed that it hadn't been one of the McCrae brothers, but it was still good.

He took a mental inventory of his weapons. He had Nita's gun, Truman's gun, and the camper's knife. He hoped he wouldn't have to use the guns. A quick kill didn't give as much satisfaction. He discovered he liked being close to the people he killed. There was something exciting about the look in their eyes the moment they realized they were going to die.

Since the court hearing he hadn't needed much money. The car had been his biggest expense. He still had more than four thousand dollars. Truman's wallet had contained fifty dollars and a few credit cards. He took the money and left the rest. He knew from watching crime shows; you could be tracked by using credit cards. He needed to lay low for a while. Being chased was exhilarating, but letting them get too close was stupid.

He stopped at a motel, one of those rundown places in the middle of nowhere, with separate cabins. When the desk clerk asked for the tag number of his truck, he explained he was delivering the truck to its owner and would be back with a different vehicle later that day. He said he'd come back in with the information. The clerk was satisfied to wait.

Bobby Ray unloaded all the gear from the truck into the room and headed for the nearest town. At a local garage, he approached the mechanic. "I need a lot of work done on this truck. Do you think you could change the oil and filters, replace the belts and hoses, service the transmission, and put on new tires?"

"That's going to take some time." The mechanic scratched his head. "We were just getting ready to close until Monday. I can't get the tires ordered until then. It'll probably be a week before they're delivered."

"That's no problem for me. I'm staying in the area for about a month. I need a little peace and quiet to finish some art work I've been working on." Bobby Ray noticed the name printed on the front of the man's shirt. "I could leave the truck with you for a week if you have one I could use as a rental, Paul."

"The only spare car I have is an SUV that we're putting out for sale next week."

"If you can hold off on selling it, I'd give you five hundred dollars to rent it for the week."

Paul looked at the car and scratched his head again. "I can't turn that down, but I would need the money for the car up front. We can settle on your repairs next week. I'm in a hurry to get home."

"Sure, just call me at the motel down the road on Friday. Ask for Jerry Bennett."

Bobby Ray handed the mechanic five hundred dollars and took the keys to the old Ford Bronco. It wouldn't be missed for a week and it had plenty of room for his gear. Hell, it had enough room for all that, plus a couple of bodies.

Back at the motel, he loaded the Bronco. He hadn't slept much lately. Watching Jordan had become a full time job. He decided to take advantage of the bed until it was dark, then he'd figure out where to hide out for a while. He closed his eyes and thought about his latest kill.

Bobby Ray was so pleased with his quick thinking action he'd rewarded himself with a box of colored pencils. The first pencil he'd noticed was the light rust color that matched Jordan's hair.

Jordan had a soft heart. She wouldn't allow too many people to get hurt before she came to her senses and gave herself up to him. He smiled at that thought as he rolled onto his side to sleep.

****

Connor looked out the kitchen window at the oak tree, remembering how Tucker had described the findings of the medical examiner over the phone. He rubbed his forehead trying to ease the ache.

Butler's camping spot had been found by the creek just a quarter mile from the back of their lawn. A clear path had been made from recent and frequent use. Rolled up gum wrappers and scuffmarks indicated the place where he'd sat watching them. Where was he now?

In the morning his father was sending a small plane to pick up John's body. Ted and Caleb would go back with him. He planned to drive Jordan and Lizzy in the BMW. The road trip would do them all good.

Ted would stay in Tampa to wait for the arrival of his first baby. Hopefully, Caleb would stay behind as well. He'd enjoyed being with his brother again. Their relationship had changed and matured since their reunion. Maybe it was because they weren't so much alike any more. He still wished he knew what caused Caleb to be so closed up. It suddenly occurred to him that he had avoided his brother for a solid six years, now he hated to think of leaving Tampa without him. But, Caleb would be safer at home.

How would he keep Jordan safe by himself? She would never consider leaving her home again. It was all she had of her past and it was Lizzy's future. They'd made it their home.

The house was quiet. In the living room Jordan sat at one end of the couch, crocheting a blanket for Ted's baby. Caleb had perched at the other end reading the newspaper. Lizzy was coloring a picture at the end of the coffee table and Ted's reading glasses had slid to the end of his nose as he worked on John's eulogy. John had left an emptiness that they all felt. This would be the last night that they'd all be together under this roof.

He climbed the stairs to the bedroom and picked up his guitar. He hadn't played it since the cookout. He couldn't let this last night go without drawing everyone together one last time.

Next, he stopped in the spare room downstairs to find Caleb's guitar. When he returned to the living room, Caleb looked up, smiled, and held out his hand for his instrument.

Connor played a few cords before Caleb settled into the same tune. Ted sang along to the old Willie Nelson song. Lizzy crawled into her mother's lap to listen. For the second song, Connor and Lizzy sang *I Never Promised You a Rose Garden*. They had practiced it while Jordan had still been working.

Connor set down his guitar and pulled Jordan up to dance with him while he sang softly in her ear.

"What would you like to sing?" he asked when the song ended. "We can play almost anything."

"I don't sing."

"Of course you sing. It's natural. You shouldn't be shy with us. We sing all the time."

"But you're so good. I can't sing. I don't even know any songs."

"You may as well get it over with," Ted told her. "They'll get you sooner or later."

"I seriously don't know the words to any songs."

"I can't believe that," Connor stated. "Don't you sing along to the radio? Haven't you ever done Karaoke? Tell me your favorite song or artist and I'll help you."

"I haven't sung since I was a kid in Girl Scouts. I only faked it then. I have a voice like a bullfrog."

"That's not true. I've heard you laugh. You can't have a laugh like that and not sing well."

Caleb came to her defense. "Give her a break, guys. You can't force her to sing. That's no fun. She's not used to being around a bunch of hams like us. She'll come around when she gets good and ready. Let's get Lizzy into this again. She can do *Who's Bed Has Your Boots Been Under*."

"What the hell are you teaching my five-year-old?" Connor exclaimed.

"Is that wrong? I don't know much about kids." Caleb couldn't hold back a laugh. "I was just kidding. What about *Mockingbird*?"

Jordan was surprised at how well Lizzy had

learned. The men finished with two soft ballads that nearly had her asleep. Jordan followed as Caleb carried Lizzy to bed.

"Do you think you can help me talk Caleb into staying in Tampa after the funeral?" Connor asked Ted.

"I'd feel better if you had back-up here. It'd be even better if you'd all stay in Tampa, just until Butler is back behind bars."

"I'm not too confident that it's going to be that easy. He found Jordan before he'd even left the prison. He'll find her again. I can't lead him to my parent's doorstep. Anyone around us is in danger. I think John proved that. I figure Bobby Ray's laying low for a little while. He'll be back, even more determined." Conner's eyes drifted toward the stairway. "It's not going to be as easy as walking up and slapping handcuffs on him. We'll have a fight on our hands. I'd bet my life on it."

"I think maybe I'll come back with you."

Connor hung his tired head and thought a minute. "Are you expecting a boy or a girl?"

"We're having a boy. Don't try to sidetrack me."

"It's okay, man. John's boy isn't going to have a dad anymore. Maybe he can help your son learn how to deal with it too. He'll be a big help to Jenny after you're dead. It's tough for a woman to raise a kid by herself, you know."

"You are an absolute prick, you know that?" Ted growled.

"Go home and welcome your son into the world. Stay home and teach him to be something better than Bobby Ray Butler. I'm going to bed. We have a long day ahead of us tomorrow."

Connor lay back on his pillow and watched Jordan

braid her hair for the night. "I like that blanket you're making."

"Yeah, it's nice and soft for the baby to cuddle up in."

"How long does it take you to make one of those?"

"That depends on how much time I've got. It could take a day or a week. Why, are you thinking of taking up a new hobby?"

"No, I'm thinking of having babies. I just wanted to make sure that they'd have plenty of those fluffy little blankets."

"I don't even want to think about getting pregnant right now. I've got enough complications in my life."

"Okay, but I hope you don't mind if I think about it. I may even want to get in a little practice."

"Well, practice does make perfect." She crawled over the bed to kiss him.

Chapter Twenty-Four

The next morning Caleb and Ted took a cab to a private airport where the company plane was waiting. Connor wished he could drive them himself, to make sure all went well. He knew he couldn't take Lizzy to watch John's body being transported, but he couldn't leave her and Jordan at home alone either. He had to trust Caleb to handle any problems.

It made him nervous to let any of them out of his sight since John's death. What had he gotten them all into? His father was right to be so pissed. Connor still hadn't heard from him directly. Ian McCrae had made all the arrangements through the medical examiner's office. Ted was the only one who'd spoken to his father since that phone call to Jordan. Connor would have to face him today. How could he apologize for what had happened to John? How was he going to face John's family? This definitely qualified as one of the worse days of his life, and it had barely begun.

Connor looked out the kitchen window as he sipped his coffee. Butler could be out there anywhere, watching.

"This is my family now, asshole," he whispered. "You'll never hurt them again. We will find you."

****

After leaving the interstate, they drove for another twenty minutes away from the city before turning into a drive. They stopped in front of tall iron gates. It seemed like the stone fence stretched for miles. Connor punched a code into a keypad by the driveway and the gates opened.

"How did you remember the code after all this time?"

"Easy, it's my birth date. Mom wouldn't ever let it be changed. She says that was the day we became a family."

"I don't even know when your birthday is."

"I can't tell you now. Then you'd know the code. That's a family secret."

"When we get married, I'll be family too."

"Okay, I'll tell you when we're married."

The house was a colonial brick with white trim. In the middle of the front porch were huge white double doors that looked small against the size of the house. The windows had to be six-feet tall. A balcony surrounded the entire second floor, looking over the spacious lawn. Connor stopped the car in the middle of the circular drive. The doors opened and an elderly black woman stepped out.

"That can't be your mom, unless you're adopted. You weren't adopted, were you?" Jordan asked.

"No. That's Miss Hannah. She helps Mom around the house. She's been with us since Caleb and I were born. I'm surprised she hasn't retired yet, but I'm glad she's here. The place wouldn't be the same without her."

"I bet she knows your birthday."

"Yes, but she's been sworn to secrecy."

Jordan stepped out of the car feeling a little shaky. She realized it wasn't Tampa that had her so nervous. It was coming face to face with Ian McCrae. She gently shook Lizzy awake. "We're here, honey."

"What is this place?" Lizzy rubbed her eyes.

"This is where Mr. and Mrs. McCrae live. I want you to be on your best behavior here. It's really important to Connor that we make a good impression. Don't run or yell or touch anything. Be polite. That lady on the porch is Miss Hannah. She takes care of the house."

Connor finished taking the few bags from the car and walked up the steps. To Jordan's surprise, he pulled Miss Hannah into a long hug. The old woman stepped back to wipe tears from her eyes. "I wondered if I'd live long enough to see you walk up those steps again. I sure have missed you." Miss Hannah reached up and patted his cheeks. "I'm sorry for the reason that brought you back, but I'm glad you're here. I heard that you were bringing your new family with you. I'm so happy for you, Mr. Connor."

Connor introduced Jordan and Lizzy. Her smile let Jordan know she had an ally in the house.

"Let me show you the rooms you'll be staying in. I'm sure you'll want to freshen up and change after such a long ride." She led them up the central staircase and to the right. "Mrs. McCrae thought Lizzy would enjoy staying in your old room, Mr. Connor. I put you and Miss Jordan across the hall."

****

Connor found his childhood room just the way he'd left it when he went away to college. Model cars were lined up on the shelves. Sports posters hung on every wall. His old baseball bat and glove leaned in the corner. The only new additions were a doll, coloring book, and crayons on the end of the bed.

"These must be for you, monkey. I don't remember having any dolls."

"Oh, this is a great room. Can I look at your picture book?" Lizzy ran her hand over an old photo album.

"No, honey, I think I've had all the nostalgia I can handle for now. You just play with your things while Mommy and I get cleaned up. Then you can get a bath." Connor asked, "Miss Hannah, where are my parents?"

"Mr. McCrae went to town to take care of a few arrangements. Your mother had a little shopping to do. She wants your first dinner at home to be special. They should be back shortly. Can I get you anything?"

"No thanks, but could you see that Lizzy gets a little lunch while we unpack and shower?"

"I'd love to." Hannah closed the door as she left.

Connor unpacked while Jordan used the bathroom, and then took a quick shower. Returning to the room he found Jordan sitting at the vanity, still wearing her robe.

"What's the matter, boss?"

"I only brought a few clothes and I don't know what to wear." Jordan held her arms out. "I didn't expect all this. The idea of meeting your parents has me a little intimidated. I want to make a good impression."

"I can guarantee that Dad will wear a suit and Mom will wear jeans or shorts. You can go either way or anywhere in between." He chuckled a little. "Believe me, there's always a lot of room in between. The two of them are as different as night and day."

"How do they get along that way?"

"They're each other's alter ego. It's interesting to watch."

"So, let me ask you, Connor…" Jordan dropped the towel she had wrapped around her. "Have you ever messed around in your parent's house?"

"I never had the nerve, until now."

The moment their lips touched, a knock sounded on the door.

"Your father is back," Miss Hannah whispered through the crack in the doorway Connor guarded from the other side. "He wants to see you in the parlor immediately."

Why did it seem like the walk from his room to the parlor was twice as long today? When he saw Ian McCrae sitting in his favorite wingback chair he could have sworn time had frozen him there. His hair was a little whiter, but he was as fit and formidable as ever.

"What do you have to say for yourself, Connor?"

"A lot has happened. I planned to go over it all with you as soon as we're settled in."

"I don't want to hear what I've already learned from reading reports," Ian snapped. "I just left John's widow picking out clothes for her husband to be buried in."

"I would never have let something like this happen intentionally. John's been like an uncle to me. I've done my best—"

"I don't know what to think of you, hiding yourself away for six years, and then resurfacing to get one of my best friends killed. Look at you. You look more like a bohemian than I did in my teens. What the hell are you thinking, son? How do you expect people to give you any kind of respect?"

"I earn it, Dad. It takes more than a suit and tie for people who really matter."

"Bullshit! You've lived like a loser for so long you've forgotten how to live like a normal human being."

Lizzy raced into the room and kicked the older man with the toe of her little sandal. "Don't you talk to my daddy like that, you mean old man!" She burst into tears. "He's the best daddy in the world."

Connor picked her up and held her as her tears soaked into his T-shirt. "She's been through enough. Maybe this wasn't a good idea. We'll find a hotel to stay at until after the funeral."

Ian McCrae looked stricken as he watched his son cuddle the little girl. "No, you should stay. I'm...I'm sorry."

Jordan walked into the room with fire in her eyes. "Connor, could you take Lizzy up for her bath please."

"Wait a minute, Jordan..."

"No, I need to talk to your father for a moment. I'll be right up." She forced a smile for Lizzy's benefit.

"Go ahead son." Ian sighed. "Jordan and I need to get acquainted. Don't worry, I'll play nice."

"The problem is, Dad, she's not playing."

"I figure I deserve it. Go on upstairs with your daughter."

"Are there any last words you'd like me to give to Mom?" Connor asked his father with a crooked grin.

"Tell her that I've always loved her."

"Okay." Connor shrugged as he walked out of the room with Lizzy.

****

"Okay, let's have it. I'm ready for both barrels," Ian stated.

"I let you bully me on the phone. Maybe you think

I'm a pushover because of that, but not where my family is concerned. I don't know what you said to upset my daughter, but I'm betting you were laying into Connor. He's sick over what happened to John. That man was closer to him than you are. You should think about that. You have two wonderful sons that you treat like shit. Why the hell did they follow in your footsteps? Think about that too. I want to get along with you for Connor's sake, but if you can't get along with Connor, why should I try? We can go back to Mayville and live very happily without you. My daughter hasn't had anyone but me for most of her life." Jordan stopped for a breath. "She was really looking forward to this visit. It's the first thing she's had to look forward to since this nightmare started. And if you think it's been a nightmare for us, try living it as a five-year-old. Now, her first impression of you is that you hate the man she loves most in the world. If you ever make her cry like that again, I'll tear you to little pieces and put you back together wrong." By the time she stopped for another breath she was just inches from his face.

"I believe you mean it."

"You need to believe it. It may be the only thing that saves you."

"What can I do to fix the mess I've made?" Ian asked. "I didn't expect her to be close enough to hear us."

"She's five, she hears everything. The truth is you shouldn't have said whatever you did in the first place. Connor has been through hell. He didn't need this, his first day back. I'll give you twenty-four hours to make up to both of them or we're out of here. How you do it is up to you."

"I'm sorry, Jordan." Ian seemed to shrink into himself.

"Yeah, I already got that impression."

"No, I really want to apologize. I'm glad Connor has a woman like you. You're strong. I can respect that. You've sure made a change in him. I can tell he has his confidence back."

"Then don't try to take it away from him again," Jordan said.

"Do you think that's what I was trying to do?"

"I don't know if that's what you were trying to do, but you were doing a good job of it anyway."

"I want my son back. I want this family to heal."

"The ball is in your court, Mr. McCrae." Jordan turned and left the room.

When she returned to their room Connor was putting the last band around Lizzy's braids. Jordan opened a suitcase and began hanging clothes in the closet. A tap sounded on the door.

"Who is it?" Connor called.

"It's me. Are you decent? Can I come in?"

"I've never been decent, but that's never kept you out before."

The door flew open and Melanie McCrae ran into her son's arms. "I can't believe you're here. You look terrific. Look at your hair. Your father must hate it. I love it. Have you had anything to eat? I'm making all of your old favorites tonight. How long can you stay? God, I've missed you," Melanie McCrae babbled.

"I've missed you too, Mom, but we can only stay for a few days."

"Are you Daddy's mom?" Lizzy asked from her seat at the vanity.

"Yes I am, sweetheart. That makes me your grandma. Is that okay?"

"I guess so, but I don't think I want to have a grandpa."

"Well, I don't think I blame you right now, but you may change your mind." She hugged Lizzy. "Will you give him one more chance to show you what a great grandpa he can be?"

"Do I have to?" Lizzy hung her head.

"No, but it would make me so happy if you would."

"I guess I can try."

Jordan watched from the door of the walk-in closet. Her future mother-in-law pleasantly surprised her. She looked to be closer to fifty than sixty-years-old. Her blonde hair was cut in a feathery short style. She had the same blue eyes and tanned skin as her sons. Her five-foot-eight, athletic form had gotten slightly soft with age. She was the type of person who smiled with her whole face, and you could tell she smiled a lot. Not knowing what to say, Jordan cleared her throat.

"Mom, I want you to meet Jordan Holbrook, my fiancée."

"Oh…" Melanie sighed as she walked over to take Jordan's hands and look her over. "So you're the woman who has stolen my son's heart."

"I think Lizzy had a lot to do with that, Mrs. McCrae."

"I can tell that he's crazy about her, but that twinkle in his eye could only have been put there by a woman. I know my sons. That one is in love. You can call me Melly. That's what my friends call me. I heard you've already met my husband. You made quite an impact on him. He's still in the parlor, licking his wounds."

"I'm really sorry about that." Jordan's face warmed.

"I'm not," Melly laughed. "He must have deserved it. I'm glad you put him in his place right from the start."

Chapter Twenty-Five

Connor was sitting on his bed looking through his high school yearbook when his father knocked on the open door.

"I need you to go over to the Truman house with me, Connor. Laura is worried about Josh. She just found him with a gun."

Connor noticed that he wasn't looking directly at him. Could he actually be sorry for the way he'd behaved earlier?

"I sure hope you're kidding, but I know you're not. What is that boy thinking?"

"I don't know, but you're better at this kind of thing than I am." Ian looked at the floor with his hands in his pockets. "Will you go?"

"I've never dealt with a teenager who had a gun before. I don't know what I could say." He stood to follow his father down the hallway.

"Well, I'd probably yell at him for a while."

"Anything is better than that," Connor scoffed. "He'd probably end up shooting you."

At the Truman house, Josh was sitting on the porch swing. His head hung down with his arms crossed, like a pouting child. But, he wasn't a child, he was nearly a grown man, and at the moment he was dangerous. A second family tragedy had caused him to backslide into a rebellious teen. Connor felt responsible; it was his job to help…somehow.

Laura Truman was nervously watching from the door when the two men got out of the car and walked toward the house. Connor sat on the other end of the swing.

Josh had grown up a lot in the last four years. He was taller and thicker. His black hair had been cut short. The only signs left of his previous rebellion were an earring and a tattoo under his T-shirt sleeve that read *Born Bad.*

"You got any coffee, Laura?" Ian asked as he guided her into the house.

Connor was silent until they'd been left alone, although he knew they'd be listening from the other side of the living room window. "I hear you've got a gun."

"Yep, and I intend to keep it, too," Josh sneered.

"What do you plan to do with it?" Connor leaned back casually.

"I'm going to kill the son of a bitch."

"I figure you mean Butler. What's your plan when that's done?"

"I don't know. What does it matter?"

"Well, I was just asking because I was thinking about doing the same thing myself not too long ago. Did you know that he's the same guy who cut me up?" Josh gasped, but Connor continued. "I wanted revenge. I thought of doing all kinds of nasty things to him, just to watch him suffer."

"Yeah, that's right. I want to see this guy squirm. So, what changed your mind?"

"I met Jordan, my fiancée, and her little girl Lizzy."

"So you fell in love and now you don't care anymore? They say women make you weak. I guess it's true."

"No, I don't think so. I started seeing myself through their eyes. It made things seem clearer. I realized I was turning into the same kind of animal he is. Listen Josh, Jordan is a stronger person than I am. Butler hurt her a lot worse than he did me, but she's not looking for revenge. She wants justice. I decided if I want to have a decent life after Butler's gone, justice is what I need, too. Then I can go to Jordan a clean and whole man. We can live our lives out happy together. You know, if an ugly ogre like me can find someone like Jordan, there must really be someone out there for all of us. Just look at my dad. He's an asshole. So what makes him deserve a woman like my mom? But she's crazy about him."

"I don't care about that shit." Josh turned his face away.

"Neither did I," Connor admitted. "But it happened. And when it happens, it suddenly becomes the most important thing in your life. If I were to let those old feelings for revenge take over, I'd miss out on so much now. Keeping my family safe is my priority. That was a big priority for your dad, too. He was a damn good man. He talked about you the last time we spoke."

"Did he tell you what a fuck-up I am?" he groaned.

"No. He said you'd been through a hard time, but that you were getting past it and becoming a man. He was proud of you, Josh."

"I don't know if I want to grow up."

"It's an awesome responsibility, but we don't have

much choice. Sometimes, I'm still not sure I'm ready. That's when I crawl into bed with my woman and let her baby me until I feel like a man again. It's so worth it, Josh. I hope you don't give all that up for someone like Butler."

"Mom wants me to be a pallbearer tomorrow, along with you, Cal, Ted, and my two uncles." Josh wiped a tear from his cheek.

"She loves him, Josh. She wants the men who he loved most to take care of him this one last time. Who else could she trust with that?"

"What if I screw up?"

"Then we all screw up, but we'll do it together." Connor held out his hand. "Now, show me the gun."

"Are you going to take it?"

"No, but I want to make a deal with you. Hand it over."

Josh reached into the waistband of his jeans to pull out the thirty-eight special. Connor was relieved he'd gotten to him before he blew his dick off. The stupid things people pick up on TV.

Connor took the gun, and before Josh knew what was happening, he emptied the bullet chambers, and then handed it back.

"Why did you do that?" Josh exclaimed.

"I want you to give me six months," Connor explained. "Then, I'll let you have the bullets back. You have my word on that, as long as you promise not to replace them until then. No matter what you decide, I'll give them back to you. It's a gentleman's agreement bound by trust."

"I guess I don't really have a choice."

"You have a lot of choices, Josh. I just want to

make sure that you think them through carefully. And, I want you to put that gun away. I don't want your mom to see it again." He held his hand out again and Josh shook it.

Ian stepped out the front door. "We'd better be getting back for supper, son."

On the way, Connor gazed out the passenger window, mentally replaying every word he'd spoken to Josh. He hoped he'd said the right things. If Josh reacted to his anger and teenage impulses it would destroy what was left of a family he loved. He made a silent vow to follow-up with the kid on a regular basis.

"You handled that well, Connor, a lot better than I would have. I would have probably sent the kid over the edge. I wish I was more like you sometimes."

Connor was amazed by his father's admission. "Sometimes I wish I was more like you. You never make mistakes. John would be at home with his family if you'd been in my place."

"From what I understand, John went out on his own. He didn't even let his partner know what he was up to. That was the mistake that cost him his life. I wish he hadn't done it, but I know he was trying to protect you. He loved you. Unfortunately, Butler was one step ahead of him. I don't know if John would have taken that chance for me. Have no doubt about it, son, I've made a lot of mistakes." Ian squeezed the bridge of his nose and took a deep breath. "You were right about what you told Josh. I don't deserve your mother, or you two boys for that matter. I am an asshole." Connor could tell this wasn't easy for his dad. "Our conversation this morning was uncalled for. I should have told you how glad I was to have you home. I should have welcomed Jordan into the family. I should have been a lot better with Lizzy. It seems like I always let my mouth override my brain. I always end up regretting it later." After a deep breath, he added, "What I really want to tell you, Connor, is that I think Jordan is a treasure. She's passionate and strong, like your mother. She'll be the best friend you'll ever have. Lizzy…what can I say? She's a little fireball. I can see that she loves you. I wish I could start over from the beginning with her. In short, I just want you to know that I'm really proud of you, son."

Connor could hardly breathe around the lump in his throat. "Thanks, Dad. I wouldn't worry too much about making up with Jordan and Lizzy. Besides being very passionate women, they're both very forgiving. I know you'll work it out."

Ian slowed the car. "Do you mind if I stop at the mall before we go home?"

"No, I guess not. I could probably use a few things myself."

Connor came home with a small bag of grooming supplies and a bottle of perfume for Jordan. Ian carried a large pink box with a white bow on top. They found the women just getting out of the swimming pool.

"What's in the box, Ian?" Melanie eyed him warily.

"A new grandpa has rights, you know," Ian answered.

"Are you seriously going to try to bribe your way into Lizzy's good graces?"

"I had to find some way to break the ice. Give me a break!" Ian looked embarrassed. "By the way, what's for supper?"

"Connor's favorites." She smiled.

"Oh good Lord, where are the antacids?"

They had supper in the large formal dining room that evening. Connor and Caleb each ate three chilidogs with cheese and onions along with a plate of onion rings. Despite the fact that Lizzy was unusually quiet in Ian's presence, she couldn't resist the cuisine.

"Why's the munchkin so quiet?" Caleb asked.

"She had a little run-in with dad this afternoon."

"Any casualties?"

"Nothing serious, but Dad has a hell of a bruise on his right leg."

"I'm surprised Jordan let him live." Caleb grinned.

"The jury is still out on that."

"Did you bring your guitar?"

"Do I go anywhere without it?"

****

Jordan helped Melanie finish clearing the table for Miss Hannah and was drawn down the hallway by the sound of music.

"You're an amazing woman, Melly, teaching your sons to express themselves so openly through music."

"Me? I made up a few songs for them when they were little, but I'm completely tone deaf." She opened the door to reveal Ian sitting at the piano. He was singing an old Billy Joel song. His voice was as clear and strong as his sons'.

Jordan was surprised to see Lizzy move close to watch his fingers play over the keys. "Are you going to open your present?" he asked Lizzy.

"It doesn't have my name on it," she replied.

"I forgot that part, but you can open it anyway."

"Do I have to?"

"Why not?" Ian tilted his head. "Don't you like presents?"

"Yes, but I don't know if I want a present from you." Her voice lowered. "You're kind of a stranger."

"What about a trade?" Ian suggested. "I'll give you the present if you'll sing a song for me."

"I can sing Mockingbird if somebody sings with me."

"I guess I can help you out."

She sat on the piano bench next to him and belted out the song in her childish voice as he accompanied her. When he handed her the box, her cheeks flushed with excitement. Jordan had never had the means to spoil Lizzy with impromptu gifts. Ian looked just as anxious. Her reaction seemed to mean a lot to him. Jordan hoped this would mark a new beginning for them.

Inside the large pink box was a big gray teddy bear wearing a blue T-shirt with *Grandpa Bear* printed across the front. In its arms was a little reddish-brown bear with a pink T-shirt that read *Lizzy Bear*. Lizzy wrapped her arms around Ian's neck and placed a kiss on his cheek.

"I'm sorry I was such a jerk, Lizzy," he whispered.

"You're not such a mean man, are you?" She smoothed his tie.

"I suppose I could be better, but I've never had a little girl to give me hugs before. I think that will make me much nicer."

Chapter Twenty-Six

For the second day, Bobby Ray watched Jordan's property from his new and closer hiding place under her house. She, McCrae, and the kid were still nowhere in sight. They'd left town, but they'd be back. Nothing had been moved out. Well, nothing except the big tree where he'd hung the investigator. A length of the rope still circled the trunk from when they'd cut it up to feed into a chipper. The memory must have been more than their poor little hearts could stand.

The old man, Arnie, supervised the twin boys unloading a bunch of wood from his truck. "That old tree was here before I was born. It's a shame it had to come down, but all things must end sometime. Maybe it'll be in a green pasture in heaven when I die. I wouldn't mind lying in its shade again."

"Don't say such things, Mr. Coleman," one boy said. They were so much alike it was hard to keep them separate when they moved around so much. Just like those McCrae brothers must have been before one was scarred.

"It's the truth, son," the old man continued. "We have to clear out and make room for the future. This old tree is gone now, but something new and beautiful will take its place."

"I wish we had more time to work today," the second boy remarked. "Do you think we'll be able to

218

get it all done tomorrow?"

"We will if we work steady all day. I want this to be a nice surprise for Jordan when she returns."

Bobby Ray was glad when they finally got back in the truck and left. As he crawled out from under the house and stood, every muscle stretched to its breaking point like old taffy. He'd learned the patrol cars' schedule. He had about half an hour before it came by again. That left plenty of time to look around.

If the old man and his boys planned to work the whole next day, chances were slim Jordan would return until the day after that. Bobby Ray would treat himself to a decent hotel bed for the next couple of nights.

He entered the barn first to find Jordan's old car and McCrae's van. The fancy sports car was gone. If he knew anything about cars, he'd cut the brake lines like they did in the movies. Maybe that only worked on twisty mountain roads, though.

He walked onto the back patio to look through the windows. Bobby Ray closed his eyes and recalled the neat, clean rooms from when he'd gone inside and found the cat. He wished he could have seen Jordan's face when she saw it. He felt that it made a clear statement, but McCrae hadn't paid attention. Jordan was his woman. McCrae should have gone back where he belonged. Too late now.

If Jordan had kept her mouth shut and stayed with him this would be his house. By all rights, it should be his. She was nothing more than a whore. She had him put in prison so she could find herself a rich man. Connor McCrae was living the life that should have been his.

Bobby Ray hiked two miles to where he'd left the

borrowed SUV, his muscles aching. The cops were probably looking for the vehicle by now, so he drove for an hour in the opposite direction from its owner. A grizzly, ill-tempered innkeeper rented him a room. It didn't matter what it looked like; he was exhausted.

Bobby Ray took a two-hour nap, showered and changed into clean clothes. He still felt restless. He walked to the motel office to get a cold drink from the vending machine.

"Hey mister, you need anything for your room?" The female voice came from the front desk. She was a young girl about seventeen-years-old, filing her nails and chewing gum. She was a very petite brunette with dark eyes. Her eyes reminded him of Jordan's. She wore only a bikini top and cut-off jeans.

"I don't remember seeing you in here earlier." He gave her an interested smile.

"My name is Donna. My dad owns this shithole. I don't really like looking after the place, but my mom took off last year. Once a week, Dad goes to town. He's on a bowling league. He doesn't get back until the bars close, but if you need to talk to him, he'll be here in the morning."

"I was just wondering where a person goes around here for some fun." He winked seductively. "Where do you like to go?"

"I don't get to go out very much. Even if I did, there ain't any fun places nearby," she answered with a coy smile.

"Don't you have a boyfriend? Where does he take you?" He moved closer to lean on the desk.

"I'm not allowed to go out with boys." She pouted. "My dad is a real pain in the ass since my sister got pregnant and took off with her boyfriend. That was three years ago. He hasn't taken his eyes off me since, except for bowling nights."

"I bet your sister knew where to have fun." He looked directly into her bikini top.

"She sure did," the girl giggled. "She told me about how she and her boyfriend used to take a six-pack down to the levy and skinny dip in the moonlight."

"Sounds like fun to me. Have you ever done that?"

"Are you kidding? My dad would have a conniption."

"You want to go there with me tonight? It could be our secret." He ran one finger down her neck and around the top edge of her bikini top. "You know, I'm an artist. I'd love to do a portrait of you while I'm here."

"Really?" Her voice sounded breathless. "Well, it is an awful hot night, but what about the motel? Somebody might come by."

"Turn on the No Vacancy sign and lock up. We'll be back long before your dad gets home. I'll go get the beer and pick you up in half an hour. Remember though, this is our secret. Don't tell anybody."

"See you in a half hour."

****

Connor laid in bed that night thinking about the day ahead of him. He knew how much Josh must dread the duty of carrying his father to his final resting place. He wasn't looking forward to it either. John had been the right hand of McCrae and Sons legal team for over twenty years. He was family. They had shared tragedy and triumph.

Jordan was sleeping more soundly than she had for

weeks. She felt safe. He wished so much that he could just take her away until it was all over. The truth was, she was a magnet for Butler. Wherever she went, he would follow. He thought of Lizzy, sleeping across the hall. She was never really of any interest to Butler. She was just a means to an end. Perhaps he could talk Jordan into leaving her with his mother for a while. He'd miss the little munchkin, but there was no safer place on earth.

He finally decided he needed something to help him sleep. He slid out of bed and pulled on his jeans. Walking down the stairway, he thought about how familiar the house still was after all these years. Even the sounds and smells of the house were the same as he remembered. He was glad to share it with Jordan. He was glad it would be a part of Lizzy's memories as she grew.

When did all these things become important to him? He'd never thought about this kind of stuff before they came into his life. Then he realized he could hardly remember living without them. And, he couldn't imagine living without them now.

Downstairs in his father's study, Connor turned on the desk lamp and poured a glass of brandy. He looked over the shelves of law books he and Caleb had studied for so many years. On the lowest shelves were photo albums his mother kept. Each album was marked by its year on the spine. They started the year Connor's parents had married and continued until last year. Jordan and Lizzy would be included in this year's album. Connor saw the last album he would have been in, and picked out the ones for the years after. He sat at his father's desk before opening the first one. As long as he couldn't sleep, he may as well catch up a little.

This album was thinner than the rest. The pictures inside were different. No family vacations and smiling faces. Mostly newspaper articles about the court cases his father and Caleb had been involved in. His mother had kept those since the day his father landed his first job as an attorney.

Several pages into the album there were a few photos of houseguests. Then a day spent at the beach. On one page, Caleb stood proudly next to a new Corvette that he must have just purchased. It was a sharp looking black convertible. Connor wondered what had happened to the car. He hadn't seen it in the garage. He figured Caleb must have gotten tired of it and sold it. The next pictures were of Caleb with a cute little blonde at a barbeque here at the house. For several more pages the blonde girl was in all the pictures that included Caleb. She must have been important to him. Maybe she was the source of his broken heart. Caleb certainly hadn't mentioned her. The last picture in the album was just halfway through the book. That was odd. His mother had always been a shutterbug. Looking closely at the last picture of Caleb with his arms around the girl, he saw she was very pregnant. They smiled happily under the banner for the Labor Day picnic. That would have been in September.

The next album contained mostly pictures of his parents at various social and charity events. Not even the newspaper clippings mentioned Caleb until halfway through the next year. There were no more pictures of the blonde.

Connor remembered asking Caleb if he had started a family, one day at the courthouse. His exact words were *Close, but no cigar.* He had avoided any further explanation. Something must have happened to the baby. Connor's heart broke for his brother's loss. He couldn't imagine that kind of pain. He wondered what had become of the girl. They'd looked so happy together.

"I thought I heard noises down here," Caleb said from the doorway. After pouring himself a drink, he sat in a guest chair in front of the desk. He looked down at the photo albums in front of Connor.

"Catching up on lost time?"

"I guess you could say that."

Caleb pulled the album on top around to look at it from his side of the desk. The album beneath it was still opened to the enlarged picture of himself and the pregnant girl. His face froze in a pale, painful expression as he stared down at it.

"She must have been important to you." Connor didn't know what else to say.

"I'm sure you didn't miss the fact that she was pregnant with my baby. That did make her pretty damn important to me."

"What happened, Cal?"

"I killed her." Caleb stood to leave.

"What the hell are you talking about?" Connor couldn't allow him to leave without an explanation.

"I really don't feel like talking about this."

"Why didn't you tell me before? This must have been about a year after I left. No one told me anything."

Caleb turned back around to face Connor. "Don't you remember, brother? You were wallowing in your own self-pity. You weren't interested in anything that was happening to the rest of us, least of all me. After all, what problems could I have, with my pretty face?" Caleb answered sarcastically. "Mom was the only one you'd have any contact with and that was after a year. She was going to tell you, but I convinced her not to worry you about it. You'd already been through enough." Caleb poured a shot of whiskey and threw it back. "Do you want to know the most ironic part? When I got to Mayville, I found out that you had avoided me all that time because of my face. And I found you with everything that I had lost. Jordan loves you so much. My daughter would have been almost the same age as Lizzy. I envied you. I would give a lot more than my looks to have my family back."

"We used to be so close. How did this happen to us?"

"Life happened to us. Bad things happen in life." Caleb poured another shot.

"Why did you say you killed this girl? I know that can't be true."

"I was responsible. Everybody said it was an accident, but I should have been more careful.

"Two weeks after that picture was taken I was driving her home from the mall. We'd been shopping for the baby. She was due in two months. It was late and the roads were wet after a big storm. We were going down the highway with the top down. I hit an oil slick on the road. My corvette spun out. After I'd hit a utility pole my legs were pinned under the dashboard. They were both broken. Brenda had been thrown onto the road and hit by another car. By the time they cut me out and took me to the hospital, she was already gone. They'd removed the baby just before she died. It was too soon for her to survive. They let me hold her. I wouldn't let them set my legs as long as my daughter needed me. She lasted thirty minutes. In that thirty minutes I thought about all the things I had done wrong. With a baby on the way I should have had a more sensible car. I shouldn't have had the top down. I should have driven slower. I should have taken better care of her. I said I love you to her occasionally, but I never told her how much I loved her. I never even asked her to marry me. I just assumed we would get married one day. There always seemed to be plenty of time. Then, that night, the time was suddenly over. The baby was so tiny. Brenda had talked about names for her, but I'd told her we'd decide later. When they asked me to give her a name at the hospital, I couldn't think of a single one Brenda had mentioned. She was gone back to God so quickly. I named her Angel, just Angel."

"I should have been there for you, Caleb. I'll never forgive myself for that." A tear slid down Connor's cheek and he wiped it away.

"I could be mad at you for that, but I'm not. You see, no one could have been there for me. I had to go through that by myself. Sure I missed you that whole time, but you couldn't have done anything to help."

"I don't know how you get over something like that. I can't imagine it."

"After five years, I've come to understand how that works. You never get over it. You just get used to it, but you think about it every day. Everything reminds you, but you learn to live with it and keep going, hoping for another chance to love like that again."

"I'm so sorry, Caleb."

"So am I, Connor." Caleb swallowed the last of his

drink. "Always tell your family how much you love them and never forget how precious they are."

Conner watched him walk up the stairs. He finished his drink then returned to his room and Jordan.

Chapter Twenty-Seven

It was past noon when the visitor Bobby Ray had been expecting knocked at his door. He threw the bed spread over the sketchbook he'd been using.

The hotel manager looked badly hung over and pissed off. He was a short, skinny man with a beard that looked like it was shaved once a week. Probably the same day he took a bath. His head was bald on top and the back hung down in a thin ponytail. He wore baggy shorts and a cotton shirt that hung to each side unbuttoned. His dirty feet sported black rubber flip-flops. His eyes were bloodshot and his teeth were stained brown from nicotine and coffee.

"I was just getting ready to come over and talk to you about checking out today. Is there anything wrong?" Bobby Ray shaded his eyes from the intruding sunlight.

"My daughter took off some time last night. I thought you might have seen her."

"Yeah, I went over to the office last night at about seven to get a soda from the machine. She was behind the desk. Are you sure she didn't just go out with friends?"

"If she did, she'll have hell to pay when she gets back. She tends to talk a lot. Did she say anything to you about going anywhere?" He scratched his belly as he spoke.

"No, she did talk quite a bit. You know how girls that age are. She was complaining about having to work. I couldn't really stick around to listen. But, I wouldn't worry too much if I were you. I'm sure she'll turn up. She seemed like a nice enough kid." Bobby Ray was suddenly inspired by an idea. "She seemed excited when that old brown van pulled in. That must have been around midnight. The loud muffler woke me up and I looked out the window. A tall guy with blond curly hair, probably about my age, was driving. She ran out to meet him squealing and hugging. I figured he must have been family or something. You know him?"

"No, can't say I do. She was excited to see the guy huh?"

"Yep, she must have known him. She yelled out his name. I don't remember it…Oh, but I remember the last name was McCrae like those two lawyers I heard about on the news. They're those big shots that came down here from Tampa. You know the type. They act like they own the world. Sorry I didn't get a better look."

"I'll sure check it out. You just leave the key on the dresser when you get ready to go. You don't owe anything anyway." He looked over Bobby Ray's shoulder. "By the way, what is that smell in there?"

"Oh yeah, I was using some rubbing alcohol and spilled the whole bottle in the sink. No need to worry. No damage done."

"Okay. Well, thanks for the information. Sorry to bother you, Mr. Bennett."

"No problem."

Bobby Ray had been busy all morning. His bags were packed except for the things he'd bought earlier. He had just one more thing to do. He picked up the box of hair bleach and a razor and walked into the bathroom. As he used the items, he discarded them into a plastic shopping bag that he planned to throw away when he stopped for gas down the road.

In the shower, he thought about the young girl from last night, Donna. She had been easier than he'd expected. He'd only opened two beers for himself, most of which he poured onto the ground behind her back. She wasn't used to drinking alcohol and the other four beers went straight to her head. She was eager to get naked and try new things. She got a lot more then she'd bargained for, but he'd enjoyed it. She'd picked the secluded area herself. No one could hear her screams. The only part of the fantasy that was off was that she hadn't been Jordan.

After he towel dried his hair, he dressed in new clothes. Bobby Ray stopped in front of the big dresser mirror to get the full effect of the changes he had made. He admired his cleanly shaved face and blond hair. He wore snug blue jeans with a western belt and black T-shirt. All the exercise was paying off with well-toned muscles. He'd have to get used to the heavy boots, but the aviator sunglasses and straw cowboy hat looked cool.

"So, a blond cowboy type is what you want, Jordan? I always aim to please."

****

Jordan had called to check on Lizzy twice before they came to the Mayville city limits. The child's excitement over a trip to Disney World with her new grandparents had put Jordan's mind at ease.

"I don't have anything to make for dinner. Why don't we eat at the diner before we get home?"

"Do you realize we've never been out alone together? It would be like a first date. The only difference is, we've already seen each other naked."

"I guess you'll be disappointed to hear that I never put out on the first date." Jordan laughed when Connor shot her a stricken look.

In the diner parking lot they ran into the Douglases as they were preparing to leave. They had a luggage box on the top of their car.

"Where are you all off to? We're just getting home and it looks like you're leaving."

Holly and Charlie looked at each other with pained expressions. Finally Charlie answered. "It's been a little tense around here all summer. I thought I'd use some vacation time and take Holly and the kids to see my parents in Ft. Lauderdale. We haven't been up there in ages. It's just a little holiday before the beginning of school."

Jordan understood that she was, indirectly, the reason for the tension they were feeling. If she hadn't come back to Mayville, Bobby Ray wouldn't have come either. Not only did she feel guilty, but she also felt a little insecure. She'd come to rely on them for moral support as well as backup for Lizzy. She could sure understand that they needed to get away for a while. She wished she could walk away from the situation.

Connor put his arm around her to rub her shoulder. When she looked into his eyes she felt as though he could read her mind. She was relieved that he took over the conversation.

"That sounds great. Lizzy is on a little holiday with my parents." He reached out to shake Charlie's hand.

"Call when you get back in town and we'll have you over for dinner."

Ten minutes later, Jordan was staring out the window when the waitress came to take their order.

"Tonight's special is stuffed pork chops with steamed vegetables. That sounds good to me. What do you think, boss?"

"Oh, umm, that sounds fine. I'll have that too." She noticed that two glasses of tea were already sitting on their table. When had he placed their drink order?

"I'm glad the Douglases were able to take a vacation. That's less people we have to worry about keeping safe. I have a feeling things are going to get back to normal any time now." He reached over to take hold of the fingers she'd been tapping on the table.

"I know you're right," Jordan said. "I was just thinking. This is my home. This is where I want to live and work and raise my family. I love this town and I love my house. I don't want to feel this dread at coming back here. I don't want my friends and neighbors to feel unsafe around me. I just can't believe that one mistake seven years ago has caused so many people so much grief."

"You didn't cause this situation, Jordan. This started years before you ever met Butler. You were just unfortunate enough to cross his path at the wrong time. No one here blames you for the things he's done. I would venture to say that a lot of people here would have your back against him." He gave her hand one more squeeze before the waitress set the plates down between them.

As they ate dinner, they discussed Lizzy's need of school clothes, planting a vegetable garden, and trading in the van and Jordan's car for a crossover. They were both desperate to find a subject that would take their minds off their current problems. By the end of the meal they were more relaxed and left the diner laughing.

Connor had just started the car when he turned the key off and looked in the rearview mirror.

"Did we forget something?" Jordan saw the confused look on his face and turned to see what had attracted his attention. A police cruiser had pulled in behind their car, blocking them in.

****

Connor rolled down the window. "What's the problem, officer?"

"Could I see your driver's license, sir?" The police officer was pleasant but serious.

"Sure." Connor reached into his back pocket. "I know I wasn't stopped for a moving violation, is something wrong with the car?" He handed his license to the officer.

"I couldn't say, sir. I have orders to bring you in for questioning. I've also called a tow truck to take your car to the impound lot." The young man was nervously tapping the license against the hood of the car.

"You've got to be kidding. You're impounding the car? Why?" Connor was serious now, also.

"You've been implicated in a crime, Mr. McCrae. I'll need you to step out of the car with your hands in front of you. I'll be taking you to the station."

"I'm sure we can straighten this out, but I can't just leave my fiancée standing out here in the parking lot. Can't she follow us with the car?"

The officer jumped as Connor opened his door to

get out. Connor and Jordan exchanged alarmed expressions.

"No, sir," the officer replied with his hand resting over the handle of his service revolver. "My orders are to have the car brought in, to process for possible evidence. A warrant will be here before they take it away. The lady will have to find other transportation." He held out a pair of handcuffs. "Please turn around to the side of the car now, sir."

A car hauler was pulling into the parking lot, heading toward the BMW. Connor knew he only had a mere moment to speak to Jordan. The situation had caught him off guard. His mind raced to figure out what to do next. He saw the frightened look on her face as she exited the car.

"Don't worry, boss, I'll have this straightened out in an hour," he said lightly. "I'll call Caleb when I get to the station. I bet he's already on his way down here anyway. You go inside and call Joyce to pick you up. Go to her place. Don't go back to the house until I come for you, okay?"

Chapter Twenty-Eight

Bobby Ray slumped down in the driver's seat of the Bronco sketching a picture when he noticed Joyce pulling into the diner parking lot. He'd decided to follow the women and see where they went. Surely they'd find a place to hide, knowing he was close. The kid wasn't with them. That was just as well. She'd be an unnecessary complication. He didn't know how long McCrae would be out of the way so he had to move fast.

Exhaustion took over as he followed them through the little side streets of Mayville. He had to hold on just a little longer. Now that Doris, Bennett, and Nita were gone, he had to do everything on his own. He'd just spent hours setting the scene in Jordan's barn that would keep the cops busy for a while. Since then he'd sat at the edge of town waiting for the happy couple to return.

It was so easy to get information in this little town. He'd approached the twin boys who worked at Jordan's house. They were riding scooters along the road after helping the old man with a project in Jordan's back yard. He told them he was a cousin to the McCrae brothers and that he'd come to help out with security. The boys told him that Jordan and McCrae would be returning from Tampa today.

Everything was falling into place nicely.

****

"Are you sure your mom won't mind my being here?" Jordan asked as she walked into the old two-bedroom apartment at the back of the beauty salon. The furniture, carpet, and drapes looked as though they hadn't been replaced since the seventies, but they were neat and clean.

"Don't worry about Mom. She hasn't been out of her room for two years. I'm going to run you a nice warm bath. We can have a glass of wine while you soak. You've had a rotten day. It'll do you good." Joyce put her purse on the end of the sofa and headed down the hall.

"You should be more careful about keeping your door locked." Jordan turned the dead bolt on the front door.

Joyce reappeared ten minutes later to direct Jordan to the bath. "You just slide under those bubbles while I grab a couple glasses of sangria. We'll have a little girl-time while we wait for your man."

For the next hour, Joyce told Jordan stories about her mother. She removed her make-up and changed into a silk kimono. Jordan was surprised at how truly beautiful the older woman was after her long blonde curls had been brushed out around her shoulders and her face was clean.

Jordan curled up on the end of the sofa wearing Joyce's white chenille robe. "So, tell me about you and Arnold Coleman."

"I wondered when that subject would come up again." She poured herself another glass of wine. "Arnie has been a friend of mine for many, many years."

"Just friends?" Jordan asked.

"I guess you could say we love each other, but we're not in love. You know Arnie has always had a thing for your grandmother. He'll never get over her. We just act as each other's security blanket."

"But why do you do it? In all those years, you could have found someone you really did love. It's still not too late."

"That was Arnie's excuse for dumping me the other day." Joyce looked into her glass.

"I'm sorry, Joyce. I didn't realize I was bringing up a sensitive subject. I've been so focused on my own problems I didn't know you two had stopped seeing each other."

Just then, someone knocked on the front door.

"Don't worry about it, kid. It was probably for the best." Joyce stood up to answer the door.

"I can't believe Caleb is here already. He must have been on his way when Connor called." She unlocked the door and swung it wide open.

****

Connor had been sitting in a room with only a square wooden table and four fiberglass chairs. The walls were a dingy gray like the floor tiles. On one side, a round clock hung on the wall. It made a swishing sound to announce each passing second. On the other side was a small window. It was too high for even him to see out. The last few rays of sunlight had disappeared long ago. A pair of fluorescent lights glared from the ceiling. He felt itchy in the clothes he'd been wearing in the car all day.

A young cop had come into the room earlier to bring a can of soda. It was barely cool then, now it was warm. He leaned in the chair as far as he could and rolled the can between his palms.

It had been almost two hours since he'd spoken to his brother. Caleb was coming back in his father's plane. He should be walking through the door at any moment. Then, perhaps they could find out what this was all about and get to Jordan.

After finding out that the police had a search warrant for her property, he'd refused to speak to them. He couldn't think about anything except Jordan's safety. He was worried sick about her, out there alone. He wouldn't be foolish enough to trust his own judgment in an interrogation. He needed Caleb. At this point, he'd be willing to sign any kind of confession to return to her.

He mentally kicked himself for not staying in touch with Detective Tucker while he was in Tampa. Maybe he would've had some idea of what this was about. The police had told him that Tucker was in the field. That had been the extent of the information they were willing to give.

Connor stood up and paced the floor just once when Caleb finally walked through the door.

"What's going on here, Caleb? They said they were bringing me in for questioning and they're searching Jordan's place right now. They act like I've committed murder or something." He was even more confused at his brother's appearance. "Those are the same clothes you were wearing last night, and you haven't shaved. Where have you been?"

"That doesn't matter right now, although I will have to borrow some clothes when we get out of here." Caleb sat in the chair Connor had vacated. "The desk sergeant said a detective would arrive any minute. I don't have a clue why you're here. You look like hell."

The door opened. Two detectives entered that Connor didn't recognize. They held up badges and identified themselves as Mullins and Dundridge. Dundridge was a tall man with short dark hair and sunken brown eyes. He closed the door and leaned against it. Connor figured he was standing guard while his partner started the interrogation. What was Dundridge expecting him to do, attempt an escape?

Mullins was the smaller man with a gray comb-over. He held a small file as he sat across from Caleb at the table. "Have a seat, Mr. McCrae. We'd like to hear what you've been doing for the last twenty-four hours."

Connor wanted to get this done as soon as possible. He sat on the edge of the chair next to Caleb and leaned toward Mullins. "Yesterday I was in Tampa, where I attended the funeral of John Truman, along with about two hundred other people. Then, I had supper at my parent's house. If their word isn't good enough, you can check with the housekeeper, Miss Hannah. I went to bed at about one o'clock. I slept with my fiancée, Jordan Holbrook, all night. Believe me, she knew I was there the entire time. We ate brunch with my parents, and then left Tampa at about two. We took I-75 and stopped for gas in Sarasota. We arrived in Mayville at around six o'clock. We stopped at the diner to eat. We spoke to the Douglases, Charlie and Holly, in the parking lot before we went inside. I was picked up as we were leaving to go home. I got here at seven-thirty and I've been stuck in this stinking room ever since. Now can you tell me what this is all about and let me go? You have to know what kind of danger my fiancée is in right now."

Mullins ignored Connor's request and asked his next question. "Have you ever heard of a girl named Donna Bass?"

Connor stared straight ahead for a brief moment while he thought. "No, can't say I have. Who is she?"

"She's a seventeen-year-old girl that disappeared from a motel about fifty miles from here last night."

"What does this have to do with my brother?" Caleb asked.

Mullins turned to Caleb. "Her body was found in your brother's van about an hour ago. It looks like she was worked over pretty good. She'd been bound, raped, and tortured. She's dead. A guest at the motel that her father owns gave the description of that van as being there last night."

"You heard his statement. You can easily confirm his alibi."

"You know, I think you're right, Mr. McCrae." Mullins stared intently at Caleb.

"Good." Caleb stood. "Do you really have any reason to hold Connor any longer?"

"No, I think we're ready to let him go. I just have one more question."

"What's that Detective?"Caleb asked.

"Where were you last night?"

Conner leaned back and folded his arms. "You've got to be kidding."

"The guest at the motel told Mr. Bass that his daughter had called the blonde man in the van, McCrae. He didn't catch the first name."

"I was with my brother in Tampa until he went to bed," Caleb answered. "Since then I've been spending time with a young lady I met in a gentlemen's club. Her name is Leah. She lives in an apartment over some old lady's garage in Ybor City. It's on Magnolia Street just off Main."

"You can't give us a last name or a full address?"

"I know, that sounds kind of bad. We were just being two consenting adults." Caleb's face turned red.

Mullins smiled, showing tobacco-stained teeth. "We've just found out how fast you can get down here when you take a notion."

Dundridge chuckled at his partner's comment. Suddenly the door shot open, nearly knocking him down. Tucker walked into the room looking steamed.

"This case has nothing to do with yours, Tucker. We have a witness."

"Did you bother to check that witness out, Mullins?"

"We have someone tracking him down in Miami right now."

"Don't bother. He was using the name Jerry Bennett. That was Butler's attorney, the one who blew his brains out on the beach." Tucker stood nose to nose with Mullins. "Did you even take a look at the kid's body in the morgue, asshole? She still reeks of rubbing alcohol, Butler's calling card."

Connor's stomach flipped. Butler had killed again and set him up to take the fall. He'd used a seventeen-year-old kid to frame him. He wanted him out of the way. He wanted him away from Jordan.

Caleb must have had the same thought. He turned to Connor. "Where is Jordan?"

Chapter Twenty-Nine

Joyce returned to the living room with tears in her eyes and Bobby Ray's gun to her head. "I'm so sorry sweetie."

"Time to come home to Papa, sugar-boo." Bobby Ray grinned triumphantly.

"Don't hurt her, Bobby Ray. She doesn't have anything to do with this." Jordan tried to stay calm. Bobby Ray looked bazaar with his hair bleached to a bright yellow color. His eyes were bright and dancing. He truly was insane.

"Well I can't leave her behind. That just wouldn't be polite. Besides, she just may come in handy." He used his empty hand to pull two zip-ties from the pocket of his jacket. "Your friend is going to tie your hands behind your back. Just turn around and hold still. If either of you try anything funny I'll pull the trigger. You know I've done worse, so don't test me."

Joyce's hands shook as she pulled the end of the plastic tie through the loop to bind Jordan's hands. Jordan's skin crawled when Bobby Ray giggled slightly under his breath.

"Do what he says, Joyce," Jordan whispered. "He didn't go to all this trouble just to kill me. There's no need for you to risk your life."

"She's right, Joyce," Bobby Ray whispered in her ear. "I only want my wife back. That's all I wanted in the first place. I'm going to take you along for a little while to buy myself some time." He placed the gun in his pocket for the few seconds it took to bind Joyce's hands with the second tie. "You believe in true love, don't you, Joyce? Jordan promised to love me for better or for worse and I intend to hold her to that." The gun was back in his hand. "Now we're all going to go through the kitchen to the back alley and get into my car. Don't make a sound. I've got nothing to lose any more."

Bobby Ray instructed Jordan to lie on her stomach on the back floorboards of the Bronco. Then he produced another zip-tie for her feet. He pushed Joyce through the driver's door and across the console to the passenger seat.

The bump between the floorboards pressed painfully into Jordan's stomach. After a few minutes, there were no streetlights passing across the windows to illuminate the interior of the car. She was fairly certain they'd left town.

Bobby Ray drove in silence. The only noise came from the car's stereo. Tears ran down Jordan's nose as a smile crossed her lips. The song, *When You Walk In* was playing. That was the song Connor had sung while they danced for the first time. She remembered his arms around her and the love in his eyes. She wondered if she'd ever see those eyes again.

****

The twenty minutes it took for Bobby Ray to drive to his destination seemed like an hour. He was so excited his heart pounded. Finally things were going his way. He had almost everything he wanted. Sure, Jordan had been his main purpose for coming to Mayville, but now he wanted to get McCrae, too. Connor McCrae had thrown roadblocks in his way at every turn. A smart man wouldn't come between a man and his wife.

He pulled the SUV behind the old wooden structure at the back of an overgrown field. The trees were dense behind the building, but he had a clear view from the front. Hardly anyone came down this old side road.

There was no electricity for lights that hung from the rafters, but he didn't need them. There was only one wall at back. The sides were opened to loading ramps. The front looked out over the field. The moonlight was bright enough to see several support beams and conveyor belts. Wooden crates were stacked against the wall and between aisles.

He pulled Joyce's hair tightly in his left hand while his right hand held the gun to the back of her head. When he had guided her to the first set of conveyors he hit her with the handle of the gun. She fell to her knees on the dirt floor. He stripped the belt from her kimono, causing it to open and leaving her body exposed. He used the belt to tie her hands to a leg of the conveyor. She looked up at him with dazed eyes.

"You know, Joyce, you've got a good body for a woman your age. Too bad you're a tramp. You deserve to be in the dirt." He kicked her in the stomach. Her breath pushed from her lungs as she doubled over. "Scream if you like. No one can hear you. I do love to make women scream."

He walked back to the car and pulled Jordan out by her bound feet. She hit the ground, but didn't utter a sound.

Knowing there was no way either woman could

run away, Bobby Ray returned his gun to the pocket of his jacket. "Come on darlin', we've got a phone call to make." He grabbed her by her arm and jerked her to her feet. "That robe is filthy," he said. He used the hunting knife he'd killed the camper with to cut the strap around her wrists. Her eyes widened. She knew he intended to remove the robe, leaving her naked.

She brought her arm around to dig her nails across the side of his face. He punched her in the jaw and she crumpled to the ground.

As he stood over her unconscious body with the knife in his hand, a memory came back to him of a night long ago in a parking garage.

****

Conner followed Tucker's unmarked car with Caleb in the BMW. Tucker had already ordered a patrol car to check Joyce's house and wait for them. The uniformed officer, Tony Markham, was standing at the beauty salon's front door when they arrived.

"I'm not getting any answer at the door, s-s-sir," the young officer said as Tucker approached "I don't have any cause to justify going inside."

"That's okay, Tony." Tucker stopped walking. "You haven't seen or heard anything strange since you got here, have you?"

"No sir, not a thing," Markham answered.

"Here's something strange." Caleb twisted the doorknob. It was unlocked. "Jordan and Joyce would both be too cautious right now to leave the door open."

"Maybe they didn't come back here at all." Tucker stepped inside.

"What's going on out there?" a weak voice called out from the apartment down the hall.

Tucker walked into the bedroom while Connor waited outside in the hall. He didn't want to scare the woman, but he didn't intend to miss a word of what she said. Anything could be a clue to where Jordan had gone.

"I'm sorry to bother you, Ms. Walker. We were looking for Joyce and her friend Jordan. Have you seen them this evening?"

An old woman was sitting in the middle of her bed, surrounded by a ruffled floral comforter. Every surface in the room was covered with images of flowers.

"Why, yes I have, Billy. Joyce brought me my tea while her friend was in the bath. I think they left with someone who came to the door about an hour later, just as Jeopardy was going off."

"That would have been at about eight o'clock," he said. "My wife never misses that show."

"The back door is standing wide open, Detective Tucker," Markham yelled from the kitchen.

"Good Lord, what has gotten into that girl?" Ms. Walker sighed. "She knows I'm a sick old woman. She can't just run off and leave me like this."

"I'm sorry, Ms. Walker, but I'm afraid Joyce and her friend may have been taken against their will." Tucker spoke gently. "We're going to do everything we can to find them. Until then, I'm going to have Tony get Mrs. Murphy to stay with you."

While he waited for Mrs. Murphy to come from next door, Connor paced the living room floor.

"Why aren't we doing something?"

"All we can do at this point is canvas the neighborhood for witnesses," Tucker said. "Tony and I can take each end of this side of the street; you and

Caleb can do the same on the other side. When that's done, we'll hit the houses across the alley. It's been two hours since they left. They could be heading in any direction. I can't even prove they left with Butler, let alone they left against their will."

"Sir, there's something out here you'll want to see." the officer yelled a second time.

Connor followed Tucker to the kitchen door that led to the alley. They found Officer Markham looking out into the darkness, pointing at the ground. "I think it may be evidence, sir. It looks too clean to have been here long."

Tucker pulled on a pair of rubber gloves before picking up a spiral bound sketchpad by the edge of the road. "Butler's name is printed on the bottom corner of the cover. And, there's a partial shoeprint on the back. It must have been kicked out of the vehicle."

"Isn't that enough proof to call out a search?" Every molecule of Connor's body was held so tightly he felt like he'd split wide open.

"Have an A.P.B. put out on Butler," Tucker ordered Markham. "Make sure everyone understands he's armed and holding two hostages. They are not to try to apprehend him. Have them call S.W.A.T. then me when he's found. I earned my masters in psychology before I entered the academy. Maybe I can get something from these pictures that'll give us a lead."

"I don't care about the stupid pictures," Connor shouted. "We should be out there looking for Jordan."

"It won't do her any good if we're looking in the wrong direction," Caleb stated.

Connor felt like punching the pitying expression from his brother's face.

Tucker flipped the book open to the first page. Connor was surprised by the detail and raw talent Butler exhibited. However the subject matter was beyond disturbing as a story unfolded in the progression of the pages. Tucker described each one.

"A hooker on a street corner with two junkies shooting up against the wall behind her."

"The hooker has red hair," Connor remarked. "And the junkies look similar."

"Here, the woman is preparing to kiss a man. There's something coming from her mouth, smoke, mist, some kind of vapor." Tucker pointed to the side of the page. "One of the junkies is shooting her up behind her knee with his syringe, and she's smiling."

"She's a junkie too," Connor observed.

"Now the man is lying at her feet. He looks like he's dead. She's laughing at him and the two male junkies are kissing."

"Jordan told you this," Connor growled. "She told you that Butler hated gays and sluts because of his phobia about germs and disease."

"Look at this one," Caleb urged. "A woman in a bathtub has cut her wrists. A little boy, sitting on the floor, is crying."

"The boy is powerless to save her," Tucker added.

The last picture shocked Connor. In it, the little boy had killed the hooker and two junkies with a bloody knife. The look on his face was pure evil.

"I don't suppose either of you know what happened to this guy's family?" Tucker asked.

"No," Connor replied. "But I think we would have heard if his killing spree started when he was a child."

"I don't think it did." Tucker tapped his finger on

the last picture. "This murder hasn't happened yet."

"So, who's the boy?" Caleb asked.

"It's Butler, or at least the way he sees himself. Powerless to control what has happened...innocent." Tucker pointed to the hooker's bloody image. "This is Jordan, a shameless, manipulating whore."

Connor dove for the detective, but Caleb held him back.

"It gets better," Tucker continued. "The two junkies are you guys, the bad influences that poison her. Butler is avenging more than a jail sentence."

"How do Joyce or John, or any of the others, fit into this story?" Caleb asked."Collateral damage?"

Connor's cell phone rang. He looked at the caller ID. The call was coming from John Truman's cell phone. "Hello," Connor answered apprehensively.

"Hey, McCrae, how's it hangin', buddy? Are you being more careful where you park your van these days?"

"Where are you, Butler?" Connor's entire bloodstream boiled with rage.

"I wanted you to hear something. Now just listen. I love this sound."

The sound of a gunshot exploded in Connor's ear. Before he could pull the phone away, he heard a woman's painful scream and Butler laughing.

Caleb took the phone from his shaking hand, but the line was already dead.

Chapter Thirty

Connor held his fists to his forehead trying to push away the sound of screaming inside his head. Was it the scream he'd heard over the phone that would forever haunt him, or was it his own mind screaming the rage that bubbled and churned in his brain? He felt as though his body would burst into flames at any moment. He had never felt this much anger and helplessness. Not even six years ago-in a parking garage in Tampa.

The phone in Caleb's hand rang again. Connor rushed to grab it before his brother could answer. "Connor McCrae speaking,"

"Connor, this is Arnold Coleman."

"I can't talk right now, Coleman. We have a situation here…"

"Something's going on out here, too, Connor."

The urgency in Coleman's voice registered in Connor's mind. "What do you mean?"

"I just heard a gunshot. Nobody hunts out this way, especially at this time of night. I've got a bad feeling about it."

"Where do you think it came from, Coleman?"

"It was in the opposite direction of the Holbrook place, past the trees to the south. I was out back when I heard it. It was a long way off but I'm sure it came from that way."

"Butler took Jordan and Joyce." Coleman gave a

low curse. "We think he may have shot one of them just a few minutes ago. He was talking to me on this phone when he did it. We're heading that way."

"Don't bother stopping here. I'm going out looking myself."

"I'm not going to try to stop you. We need all the help we can get."

Connor relayed the conversation to Caleb and Tucker. He finished by asking. "Is there any place out in that direction he would take them?"

"There's nothing south of Coleman's house until you get to the Indian reservation. He wouldn't be able to hear a gunshot from that distance."

"There is one place." Mrs. Walker shuffled her way down the hall leaning on a cane. "Old man Jackson used to grow watermelons out that way. His field was off County Road 19. They crated and shipped them out right about this time of year. Nobody's used that old watermelon shed since he died over thirty years ago."

"Are you sure about this, Ms. Walker?" Tucker asked.

"Get the hell out there and find those girls," the old woman demanded before slumping into an easy chair.

****

Jordan came to when she heard a gunshot. Her hands were bound above her head where she hung from a support beam in the middle of the structure. Her shoulders ached from her own weight. Her robe was gone.

Behind her, Joyce was crying. She might be injured, but at least she was still alive.

Bobby Ray lean against Jordan's back, pushing her harder against the wooden beam. He inhaled the scent of her hair as he ran his fingers along her sides. "I've always loved the way you smell." His lips touched her shoulder blade. "Isn't it nice to be together again, Jordan? Tonight I'm going to show you how much I've missed you. You know what I have to do first, though. You've been a very bad girl."

Jordan couldn't hold back a whimper when his belt slid out of the loops of his jeans.

"Damn baby, you're making me hard already."

She gritted her teeth as the belt struck her back. Each time the leather landed on a different strip of flesh. Her body thumped against the beam with each strike. She felt as though her arms would rip away at her shoulders. Her entire backside burned like fire.

Joyce had screamed protests until her voice went hoarse.

Jordan's head was jerked around by the fistful of hair in Bobby Ray's hand. "Just look at what your friend has done. She's bled all over the place. I'm going to the car, but I'll only be gone for a minute. Would you please tell her how I feel about this kind of mess?"

He returned a few seconds later with a box. He pulled out a bottle of rubbing alcohol and twisted off the cap.

"No, Bobby Ray! Please don't!"

"Don't worry, baby, I've got enough for everybody." He smiled widely as he poured the entire bottle over the bullet wound in Joyce's left shoulder.

Joyce gasped before she passed out.

In a way, Jordan was relieved. Now, maybe he'd forget about Joyce and she'd make it out of this alive.

Two pairs of headlights shot around the curve of the road. The first had a flashing blue light in the front window. They drove straight across the field, not bothering with the dirt paths. The headlights bounced forward until they were within twenty yards of the shed. That's when a shot rang out a few feet from Jordan's ear.

****

Caleb was behind the wheel of the BMW when Connor pulled a handgun from the glove compartment.

"What am I supposed to do? I didn't even think about needing a gun."

"Just stay close to the car. Before this is over you may have to run the son of a bitch over with it." Connor checked to make sure his clip was full. "They jumped out, leaving their doors open, and ran to the back while Butler took two more shots. Connor was afraid to shoot without taking careful aim. Bobby Ray would have both women close to him. They squatted in the weeds and peered over the hood of the car. A low and dangerous growl came from Connor's throat when he spotted Jordan hanging naked with her back to them. Red and purple welts striped her body from shoulders to knees. He jumped up to run to her.

Caleb grabbed his shirt and wrestled him to the ground. "If you run out there he'll shoot you, Connor. Then what good can you do her?"

Tucker scurried from the back of his car to where Caleb laid across his brother. "You try something that stupid again and I'll lock you in the back of my car. We've got to play this smart if we're going to get those women back alive."

The scuffle behind the cars had given Butler time to untie Joyce from the conveyor. He held her in front of him as a shield. "Somebody is going to die here tonight, gentlemen. Who and how many is up to you. I make all the rules. First, I'm willing to trade this tramp for Connor McCrae. He has to strip down to his shorts so I know he's not armed. He walks over here with his hands in the air and a pair of handcuffs. I'll send her back to you with no more holes in her. One of you can leave with the woman. It's up to you which one. Then I'll give the man left the instructions for the next trade. I'll give you two minutes to talk it over."

Crouched behind the car, Connor handed his gun to Caleb and pulled his shirt over his head. "You get Joyce in this car and drive away, Cal. Tucker is trained and experienced with guys like this. That'll give me two less people to worry about. Meet the ambulance on the road."

"I can't just hand you over to that lunatic, Connor. There has to be another way." Caleb turned to Tucker with a helpless expression.

"I'm sorry, Caleb. Your brother's right. Head the other cars off. Have them turn off their lights and sirens and tell them to come in on foot through the woods. If Butler sees them he'll kill Jordan first." Connor watched Butler's smiling face as he walked toward the shed. He tasted the bitter hate and anger in his throat.

Joyce clutched the front of her kimono closed and staggered toward Connor. She stopped as she came alongside him. "I'm so sorry, Connor." Her voice shook.

"Don't you worry, honey. I'm going to try my best to send Jordan back to you safe and sound. If I don't get to come back with her, I want you to promise to take care of her for me, okay?"

She looked down and nodded as she began to cry

then continued toward the cars.

Butler was holding his gun to Jordan's head.

"Climb up on that crate and cuff yourself to that rafter. Then, I'll trade Jordan for your cop friend." He reached up with his free hand and slipped her wrist strap off the hook she'd been hanging from. "As soon as you're done, I'll cut her feet loose so she can walk to the car and drive away."

Smug satisfaction spread across Bobby Ray's face while Connor obeyed his instructions. Then he kicked the crate from under Connor's feet and turned to Tucker with Jordan as his shield. "Lay the gun down and strip to your shorts. Walk this way. Jordan can leave in your car when you get here."

Tucker undressed, his expression a mixture of disgust and suspicion. Like Connor, he held his hands up and walked forward.

"I lied." Butler pulled the trigger.

****

Jordan screamed as Tucker jerked back and fell. The world spun and tiny bits of dirt, shell, and rock imbedded into her bruised and bleeding back. Bobby Ray had shoved her down. She could see Connor hanging from the beam. Sweat coated his straining muscles. No matter how hard he tried, he wouldn't be able to avoid a bullet. Her mind began to slip into that safe place that had been her refuge six years ago.

Bobby Ray laid his gun on the conveyor and knelt between her legs. He slapped her hard across the face. She raised her hands in defense; the moonlight glittered off her diamond. She couldn't let Connor die. She couldn't leave Lizzy alone in this monster's world. She had to fight. But how? He was stronger and she was in so much pain.

When Bobby Ray grabbed her hand and tried to pull the ring off, she brought her head up and spit in his face. He jumped to his feet, screaming and wiping his eyes with his shirttail. "Look what you've done, you disgusting bitch!" He grabbed the gun from the conveyor.

Jordan rolled under the belts. A deafening blast sounded from the field. A crate by the wall exploded from the shot. Bobby Ray crouched behind the belt stand next to her.

"You may be a crazy old man, Coleman," Bobby Ray shouted toward Tucker's car, "but you wouldn't risk shooting one of your friends."

Bobby Ray brought his gun up to take aim. Before he could pull the trigger, he fell to the ground beside Jordan with Connor on top of him.

****

"Only a true idiot would let a man handcuff himself and expect him to actually do it." Connor dangled the set of cuffs for Bobby Ray to see before snapping them on the murderer's wrists.

"You may have the upper hand now, but you'll remember me every time you look in the mirror," Bobby Ray snarled. "Did you think I wouldn't remember that night in Tampa? My mark will be on your face for the rest of your life."

"But, look at it my way, Butler. Jordan and Lizzy will love this face while your ass sits in prison for the rest of *your* life." He leaned down close to Bobby Ray's ear. "I wonder who'll be loving you."

The sound Bobby Ray made was half-scream, half-growl. He twisted ineffectually beneath Connor's weight.

"It sure felt good to shoot my daddy's old gun again." Coleman knelt to attend to Tucker. "It looks like the bullet passed right through his side, nothing important was hit. He'll live."

"I appreciate the help, old man," Connor shouted. "You were the perfect distraction. But, dammit, you could have gotten yourself killed."

"It would have been worth it," Coleman replied. "And, unlike you, I didn't have anything to lose."

The sound of loud voices poured from the trees. Spotlights lit the scene. Despite the pandemonium that quickly ensued, Connor's only concern was the woman in his arms.

Epilogue

Bobby Ray Butler was sentenced last week to five consecutive life sentences on multiple counts of first degree murder, attempted murder, kidnapping, and various other charges. He's being transported to Florida State Prison today by the Lee County Sherriff's Department.

On a lighter note, the Arnold Coleman Memorial Park will open this weekend, thanks to the McCrae family, and the support of our local citizens. We hope everyone will turn out Saturday for a barbeque lunch, craft booths, and games. All profits will be donated to the American Cancer Foundation.

Connor clicked his truck radio off before he opened the door for Lizzy on her last day of kindergarten. He was content in the knowledge that she and Jordan carried his name, and they'd never have to worry about Butler again.

"Are you ready to meet your new brother?"

When they arrived at the hospital, the room was crowded with more family and friends than they'd ever expected. People no longer stared at Connor's scars as they waved and shook his hand on the street. He was just another citizen of Mayville.

He kissed Jordan tenderly before taking the baby from her arms. "We're naming him Coleman John McCrae. But, we'll call him Cole."

"Cole McCrae, attorney at law. Sounds good." His father grinned.

Caleb patted his shoulder before leaving the room. Connor knew his brother was happy for him, but the event had brought back painful memories.

"I wish Arnie and John could be here to see this," Joyce sniffed.

"They are," Jordan assured her. "I'm sure they'll both be watching over us for a long, long time."

A word from the author...

From childhood I've moved from place to place, from Indiana to Florida, stopping in several places in between. I also moved from job to job; as a waitress, soldier, retail manager, dental assistant, etc. The one thing I never had to leave behind was my imagination.

Storytelling has always been my favorite way to pass time. I've often been told I should write a book. Finally, I did. It was so much fun: I feel I must write more.

I've been a student of Long Ridge Writers Group and once won a short story contest with Harlequin.

I currently live in north Florida with my husband, whom I torture with crazy story lines and half written manuscripts.

Visit me at:

http://www.sandradailey.blogspot.com
http://www.facebook.com/sandradailey.author
http://www.twitter.com/sdaileyauthor

~*~

Other Sandra Dailey titles
available from The Wild Rose Press, Inc.:

THE CHIEF'S PROPOSAL
(Amazon rated 5 stars)
TWICE THE TROUBLE
(Amazon rated 4.5 stars)

Thank you for purchasing
this publication of The Wild Rose Press, Inc.
For other wonderful stories of romance,
please visit our on-line bookstore at
www.thewildrosepress.com.

For questions or more information
contact us at
info@thewildrosepress.com.

The Wild Rose Press, Inc.
www.thewildrosepress.com

To visit with authors of
The Wild Rose Press, Inc.
Join our yahoo loop at
http://groups.yahoo.com/group/thewildrosepress/

www.ingramcontent.com/pod-product-compliance
Lightning Source LLC
Chambersburg PA
CBHW070332260626
47160CB00003B/1015